MW01717199

Emotionally Charged

By Selina Fenech

ISBN: 978-0-9871511-3-1

First published 2011

DEDICATION

To my baby, due to arrive into the world not long after this book. I can't wait to meet you.

CONTENTS

PART 1

HERO ME

I stared at the crack that ran up our living room wall. To my parents, it meant insurance claims and dealing with dodgy contractors for repairs. To me it meant excitement. The crack gave me shivers like it was carved up my spine.

The ground rumbled under my feet and I shared a look with my parents, all three of us ready to bolt out of the house again. The aftershock passed before we could move. Just the last little ripple after the wave.

We've always known our town was near a major fault, but it's one of those sleepy fault lines that doesn't do anything for decades, centuries even. Then just when everyone in our middle-class paradise had achieved a false sense of security it throws a big earthquake at us. There had been a small tremor when I was a baby that I can't remember. This latest, just after my seventeenth birthday, was a magnitude 6.8. It rocked my world in more ways than one.

Dad talked on the phone to his cop buddy to get all the updates. He repeated the news out loud for Mom and me to hear.

"Power's out everywhere, and Terry doesn't think they'll get it back on any time soon."

Mom had already gathered up her collection of scented candles and lit them. Her first course of action in any blackout. The whole room smelled of struck matches and ylang ylang.

"Mom, it's not even dark yet."

"Better to have them lit now then try and do it in the dark," she said, lighting the last one.

Dad put his hand over the phone and looked at Mom seriously. "Terry says there have been reports of people looting."

Mom paused a moment, then stamped into the kitchen and picked up a brush and dustpan. "The kind of person that would take advantage of a situation like this deserves their own personal karmic earthquake."

Looters, huh? I raised an eyebrow in consideration. If there were bad guys out there, could there also be heroes? Here's my guilty secret. Mom's always pushing me to follow my dreams, but the only things I wanted were all fantasies. Falling in love with a superhero, escaping to a fantasy world with a fairy prince, being adored by a morally vague vampire, any of the above. In real life terms, I didn't know what I wanted. I just knew if I ever got a chance to follow my fantasy dreams I'd be there with bells on. Real life was kind of dull, and maybe an earthquake wasn't the romantic escapism I normally went for, but I could work with it. Even a sexy fireman would suffice.

I squatted down next to Mom where she worked at brushing up shattered ornaments that had fallen from our shelves. Her collection of ceramic owls would never be the same. I helped pick up the few which had broken into larger pieces and put them aside. Mom loved her owls. Maybe some could be glued back together.

Dad's news report continued. "We were lucky. A lot of people have lost homes. And the old post office is flattened, but we've been expecting it to fall down for years. How many times did I try to tell the council to get it renovated?"

Mom counted on her fingers and Dad mimed laughter while he listened to the phone again. "There's a shelter being set up in Livvy's high school for anyone whose house is unsafe."

I bet they needed volunteers. The shaken world felt full of possibility and I had to get out there. Even handing out blankets had my mind brewing up romantic dreams of adventure.

"Mom, can I go and help at the school?"

Mom looked up at me. A glow of pride and the darkness of worry showed all over her face. I could read the emotions clear as subtitles. For as long as I could remember, I've been able to see an energy shining from a person with their emotions. Not like an aura or anything; that sounds so New Age crazy. I'm just good at knowing how people feel. Always have been. When I was a kid I used to dream of dressing up and being a real caped crime fighter, Awesome Olivia. Then I realized reading someone's feelings wasn't the kind of power to go looking for fist fights with. But it did come in handy sometimes.

I pre-empted the inevitable worried-Mom speech with soothing words. "I'll just be helping out in a shelter, under the watchful eye of aid workers, responsible adults and doctors. Probably the safest place at the moment, right?"

"You know I like to let you do what you want, but things sound pretty rough out there. I don't want you to get hurt." She looked at the dustpan and brush in her hands as though making a point about the damage the earthquake did. Her startling blue eyes turned back toward me. Why couldn't I have inherited those? My eyes were brown instead, to match my hair which she wouldn't even let me dye. Harsh chemicals didn't fit her idea of green living.

I could win this debate though. "Just think how appealing it will look on my college application as an extracurricular activity. And I can swing past your shop and make sure it's okay."

Mom's expression brightened. "I hope there's not too much damage. I just had a porcelain shipment come in. I'd go check myself but there's so much to do here. All right, off you go then, but be careful."

Dad finished his phone call and kissed the top of my head when I stood up, his moustache tickling my forehead. "I think it's a beautiful idea, Livvy-bear. Good on you for wanting to help out."

Mom walked over to empty her dustpan, sighing as shattered owls tumbled into the trash. A pink one rolled in and I knew it was her favorite. Dad gave her a hug as though they were standing by the grave of a beloved relative. I saw how sad Mom was and gave her a peck on the cheek before I threw on my red trench coat, phone, keys and wallet already in the pocket and headed for the door.

"Buses are still running, Livvy," Dad called out. "There's a clear route to your high school. Just a couple of hours, okay? Be safe and remember curfew!"

This. This is what I was made for. I felt like I was actually glowing or vibrating, or something.

"Bless. You're just an angel." A woman with a cloud of white hair patted my hand as she took a blanket from me. She smiled, but I felt the tremble in her palm and sensed her fear. It made me tingle.

I felt like some kind of weirdo. These people were here because their homes were too unsafe to stay in, or gone entirely. I saw fear and sadness on every face and there I was, bubbling over on some kind of weird high. What was wrong with me? I felt it before I'd even reached the shelter. On the bus ride a buzz built in me the closer I got to the school and it'd been non-stop since.

Trevor, the coordinator for the shelter, was also my high school history teacher. Any other day he was Mr. Jones, but today he insisted on being Trevor. He leaned on a bench next to me and pushed the sweat up off his forehead and back over his head, slicking graying hair away from his face. His voice came out as a long sigh.

"I wish I still had a teenager's stamina. You sure you don't need a break? You've been at it for hours."

Hours? It felt like twenty minutes, tops. I wasn't sure how many blankets I'd handed out or how many people I escorted into the gym, finding them a patch of ground to rest. Any injured went straight to the hospital, but I still felt like a warrior helping out in the aftermath of a battle. I'd listened to stories, dragged restless children back to their parents, and helped unload cartons of bottled water the local U-Mart trucked in. The cartons felt feather-light I was on such a high. *I'll probably be aching tomorrow.*

I pulled my phone from my pocket for the first time and saw it was half past eleven. I also saw three missed calls and two texts from my mom. Maybe it wasn't me buzzing, just my phone doing its vibro-dance in my pocket.

Trevor watched me with concern as I grimaced. "Sure you're okay?"

"I'm fine, as long as my parents don't kill me." I tapped the screen to call them back and got nothing but failed calls. No bars on my phone meant no signal. The messages left by my parents were all from back before seven o'clock. The last bus ran at ten-thirty, and thanks to my parents' hippy car-free household policy, last bus translated to curfew and I knew it. I was going to find myself at the wrong end of a serious lecture, assuming I could find a way home.

Trevor watched my hopeless phone poking. "Phone towers have battery backups which work for a couple of hours, but in a long blackout like this they will have cut out by now."

Even if I could get through, I had no way to get home that wasn't going to put out the neighbors, or worse, Dad's cop friend, Terry. I cringed. Not the way I wanted to arrive home, and there was something about Terry that gave me the jeebies. Maybe I could stay in the shelter for the night. I just had to let my parents know I was here and safe.

Mr. Jones sighed and I wondered how good he had become at reading emotions in his time as a teacher. The amount of irritation he showed said he already knew he had another occupant to fit in tonight.

"Sorry Mr. um… Trevor. I sort of missed my ride home."

"Yes, fine, you can stay here if you can find a spare bit of floor. Landlines are still working if you want to use the phone in the office to let your parents know. Briefly. Have to keep the line clear for official calls."

"Do you think, maybe, you could call them for me?" I hated talking on the phone at the best of times. I couldn't see people's reactions, couldn't tell how they were feeling and always ended up saying the wrong thing. And now was far from the best of times. "It would just be better if a teacher told them, instead of me."

And yes, I was also dodging the lecture.

Trevor rubbed his forehead, the pen still in his hand marking it blue. He added my name to his clipboard. "Go on. I'll call them. School's off for the week and people are going to be here a while, so if you want to help out again tomorrow everyone would appreciate it."

Sounded like an offer I couldn't refuse. I nodded gratefully and he left for the office to make the call.

I still had my phone in my hand, and voice mail was down so I checked the texts my mom left. The earliest must have been while I was still on the way in, just Mom reminding me of the bus schedule. The next, five minutes after the first, asked me to check the boxes of new stock that had just arrived at her shop.

Missed the bus home *and* I had completely forgotten to go past her shop on the way in. *I can't believe I spaced so bad. The winner of daughter of the year? Not me.*

I could still go now. Heading out onto the streets seemed a bit crazy but I really wanted to do this for Mom. Knowing whether her "Duck Egg Blue" home-wares boutique was okay would mean a lot to her, especially after she lost her owls. Her little boutique wasn't far from school. Normally a twenty minute walk, but tonight I felt like I could fly.

Another family trudged into the hall armed with pillows and suitcases, prepared to camp out with everyone else, looking sad and lost. I felt bad for them, but knew they'd be taken care of at the shelter. I needed to check on Duck Egg Blue before it got any later. I slipped past them and jogged out the school gates and onto the street. The chunky heart pendant I wore thudded on my chest like a second heartbeat.

Power was still out and with it all street lights. For some reason the details of the older terrace housing which backed the main street appeared clearer than I'd ever seen before, even in the dark. It was like I could see clearer than normal. I almost giggled at how good I felt and then thought how strange it was, that I could feel good even in the midst of such chaos.

Slowing my pace, I enjoyed the excitement of the solitary darkness. So I got a bit over-excited tonight and missed my bus, but I helped people tonight and it felt amazing. Mom would understand. She was always understanding and encouraging. Checking her shop out was the least I could do.

She loved her shop like she loved her owl collection. When I was younger she talked about getting a real owl. I'd looked at her like she was crazy. "Ew no, so messy! You have to feed them real meat. So difficult."

"Life should be like that. Difficult, messy, and real," she'd replied. "You have to do what you have to do to make your dreams come true."

So maybe it was crazy I wanted a rich, handsome prince to sweep me away to far-off lands of adventure, intrigue and decadence. But I didn't want my life in half measures. I wanted real affluence, real excitement, real romance. Mom's dreams came true, and I wanted to be as happy and in love as her and Dad one day.

On the main street the shops were all still standing. Some had cracks running up pastel painted fronts, splitting quirky logos with their jagged smiles. The arty mosaic archway leading into the boutique district had crumbled, blocking the road so cars were unable to pass. *What a mess.*

A lot of windows were broken, spilling glass onto the street and making the displays sparkle as though the shabby chic furniture or gourmet cupcakes had been sprinkled with diamonds.

Then I noticed it wasn't just a lot of windows. It was every window. I figured it made sense the earthquake broke glass, but just around the corner I hadn't noticed windows broken on the rows of townhouses.

Already alert, I froze when a beam of light shone out of a building up ahead. I didn't need to see the exact pastel shade of the shop to know it was Duck Egg Blue. The light jiggled then vanished. The sound of shattering porcelain echoed in the street followed by a boy-like chuckle.

"Hey!" The word came out before I stopped to think. "Hey, get out of there!"

That was my mom's shop. The hell I was going to let someone trash or loot it. Getting called out would make them run away, right?

The possibility it wouldn't only struck me when five teen boys in hoodies jumped out through the cleared window, bringing with them an avalanche of retro dinner sets from the display. I cringed as they smashed on the pavement. I didn't recognize the guys from school, and they didn't dress like boys from this area either. More like guys from the housing estate a couple of 'burbs over who sometimes crashed parties around here. One or two held flashlights, shining them my way.

Sure they might be a few years younger than me, and I stood taller than a couple of them, but it was still five scary poors-ville thugs against one. Why did I feel like I could deal with this? The fizzy high I was on had my confidence up and blocking the part of my mind that knew this could be dangerous and that feeling invincible could just make it worse. A point proved when the boys headed for me instead of making a guilty dash.

"Stay back, I have pepper spray." I bluffed, reaching my hand into a pocket of my trench coat. I grabbed for my phone instead, swiped it on, but couldn't dial on the touch screen without looking. What would they do if they saw me dialing? Back off, or advance faster? It didn't seem worth the risk when I wasn't sure the emergency number would even redirect and work with most of the network down.

"I eat that stuff on my breakfast," one of them joked.

I took steady steps away as the boys came closer. I couldn't see their faces, shadowed under tightly drawn hoods. Every one dressed in black, like they were in uniform. There were no distinguishing features visible apart from slightly varying heights.

"I'll call the police."

"Relax, we're just out for some fun." The chuckle in this one's voice sounded like the same one who had been laughing at smashing things in Mom's shop. His idea of fun worried me.

Glass crunched on the concrete footpath behind me and I spun around to find one of the boys had snuck up on me. He made to grab for my arm and I stepped out of his way.

Anger shone from him and my body flared with adrenaline. The five of them penned me in and took turns pushing at me or grasping for me. Somehow I managed to slip and dodge through their attempts to pin me down.

The more I avoided them, the more I saw the anger in them build. No one had ever been this mad at me before. It scared me.

"Someone help!" I cried out, but my voice was lost in the wide street. I doubted anyone would hear.

I ducked under a wide swing from the closest guy, meant to hit me rather than hold me. Remembering my self-defense class, I pulled my keys out of my pocket in one hand and phone in the other. I made a wild jab at his chest with my longest key while I looked at my phone screen, thumbing in an emergency call. The key sank into flesh, startling me. I didn't expect to break skin at all. In shock as my hand warmed with the guy's blood, I paused too long and was shoved in the back. I fell flat on my face. My dropped phone skittered out of reach. On the ground, I recalled the second part of the self-defense lesson emphasizing the importance of not pissing off your attackers.

I barely felt the fall, but when I tried to call for help again there was no air in my lungs.

One of them grabbed my shoulder and rolled me over. I took his hand in both of mine and twisted. I swear I heard bones break. I also thought I heard footsteps approaching, fast. I might have just been hearing things. Just wishful thinking as the guy cradled his wrist, called me something I won't repeat and kicked me in the side of the head.

I blacked out for a bit. Sounds of scuffling faded in and energy surged through my body. Snapping my eyes open I watched a new man in a white, buttoned down shirt throw one of the hoodies against a power pole. Actually picked him up and threw him. The others were already running, or stumbling, away.

The last kid slumped against the pole. Dusting his hands, my savior turned around to reveal the face of a male model. His shirt accentuated his v-shaped chest like it had been tailored and his blond hair sat perfectly as though he hadn't just dealt with a bunch of looting delinquents. His sleeves were rolled neatly below his elbows, and although he only looked about twenty, the watch on his wrist was expensive. I'd seen it in classy magazine ads.

"Are you all right?"

Even his voice was dreamy.

I tried to sit up so I wasn't so awkward and prone, wanting to be more presentable for this god-like figure. "Hngh. Ow. Crap."

Damn it.

The guy chuckled, and his smile made my heart jump. When he grabbed my hands and helped me up with perfect care, I thought my heart would lose it entirely.

"You were amazing," he said, bending to collect my phone and keys from nearby. "When I heard someone calling for help, I came as quick as I could. Saw most of the fight while I ran down the street. I thought you had them dealt with on your own for a minute. Very impressive."

I groaned. "Impressive like a high-jumping lemming."

He handed my phone and keys back to me, giving me a scrutinizing look. "But really, how do you feel?"

How did I feel? I'd just been thrown on the ground and kicked in the head, but actually I felt… "Good? Does that mean I'm in shock?"

"Maybe. Maybe something better. My name is Jake." He took my hand, gently cleaning blood off it with a tissue and I forgot to ask what was better or whether I needed a blanket and hot chocolate in case it was shock.

"I'm Livvy," I replied, without stuttering, which was a miracle.

"Let's find you somewhere to recover then, my lovely Livvy."

Guys had tried calling me that before and it always sounded corny until now. This guy's voice was so tasty I could lick it. He looped my arm in one of his like a Victorian gentleman and I trotted obediently alongside him. It would have been a lie if I said I didn't pretend to need the support more than I did, just to squeeze a little closer. I was going to make the most of this, in case I woke up and discovered it was a concussion induced dream. Or simply that he was just being nice. *Of course he was just being nice. Someone like him wouldn't be interested in someone like me.*

We walked to the end of the street and sat at a bus stop on the corner. It was beautiful--a real work of art. Designed to bookend the fallen archway at the other end of the strip, the heavy concrete bench was covered in colorful mosaic tiles.

My mind refused to help me out with anything to say. Jake kept looking me over, and I read amusement and satisfaction all over him. He broke the silence which felt like forever, more likely only seconds long.

"I bet you feel better than good, don't you?"

I shrugged. I did still feel pretty tingly. "I think I've been on an adrenaline kick most of the night."

He chuckled. "Getting kicked like you did, you aren't surprised you're already feeling okay? You don't realize how fast you were moving back then, do you? And did you know you almost ripped that guy's hand off?"

"I did *what*?"

"It's okay. It was self-defense." Jake paused for a moment. "What if I said you are more than normal? Something different, better, possibly even supernatural? Would you freak on me or-"

"Would I think it was a dream come true? The latter." I nodded with wide eyes, waiting to see what he'd reveal. I half-expected he was setting me up for some grand punch line, but there was an energy in the air I couldn't deny. A magic I wanted to embrace. And if this guy had the key to that? Dream. Come. True.

Jake pointed his finger at my chest and then his. "You, me, we have superpowers."

I eyed him up and down, looking for outward signs of mental illness. But I felt his sincerity and wondered if this is what I'd been waiting for my whole life. If by some miracle my dreams were about to become true.

"Okay. That sounds great and all, but this is a bit outside the realm of real life. I'm going to need some kind of proof to be onboard here." *Please have proof. Please have proof. Please have proof.*

He raised a perfect eyebrow. "How about a visual demo?"

Jake took my hand and pulled me off the bench. Turning back to it, he gave it a swift kick in the center. The bench cracked down the middle and fell inward in a kaleidoscope of tiles and crumbled concrete. As completely destroyed as the archway down the road. The bookends matched even more now.

I stared, mouth open, and he waited for my response with a smile.

"Where are we supposed to sit now?" I giggled, edging on hysteria at the scope of what was happening. "And also, what the how?"

Down the road, headlights broke through the darkness and a car swung around the corner, heading down the street. Jake waved at it and turned back to me.

"You're like me, like us." He gestured to the car, speaking fast as it approached. "You've always been able to read people's feelings, right? You feel stronger when people are angry, or full of energy when others are scared. When emotions surround you, you think faster, move faster, heal faster."

I found myself nodding to his words, realizing what he said was the truth. This wasn't just a dream. I'd always been like that. My one unique feature, hidden on the inside, was more special than I had ever realized. His words repeated in me. *You're like me, like us.*

"It's real. I can tell you feel it. We're Empaths. That's why I'm here. We're always on the look-out for other people like us, and the easiest time to find them is during a natural disaster when emotions are heightened. It's often the first time Empaths really experience their power, like you have tonight."

The black SUV skidded to a stop beside us and the front side window opened. I couldn't quite see inside but heard a man talk. "We've been driving round looking for you for ages. What's the deal, Jake?"

Jake tilted his head to me and simply said, "Got one."

A girl not much older than me burst out the back door. "You really found one? Zomigosh, it's a girl!" She squealed and came toward me through a gust of shimmering red hair flying around her from her leap out of the vehicle. The front doors opened and two guys stepped out. Every one of them looked stunning. I made an effort to keep my mouth from hanging open.

I reached out a hand to the girl to introduce myself and she wrapped her arms round my shoulders, hugging me as she jittered a little dance. "I thought I might have been the only one. Don't get me wrong, I love my boys, but I've been dying to find another girl 'path."

Jake cleared his throat. "Everyone, this is Livvy. Liv, that's Emma, over there's Donny." He nodded to the tallest guy, whose velvety black skin rippled with muscles which barely seemed to fit under his clothes. "And this jerk is Jamie." Jake grinned at the last guy, a few years younger than all of them. He and Jake looked like they could be brothers. Jamie smirked back at Jake and shook my hand. Donny just nodded silently.

"So, you guys come to natural disaster areas to help out, and hope you find more people like you-like us?" I couldn't believe I was talking to a team of real life superheroes. I needed to sit down but the bench option had been removed.

"That's pretty much what we do," Jamie said.

"How did Jake find you? How long have you known what you are? Did you already know? Are you from around here?" Emma overflowed with questions and I couldn't find a gap to answer any.

Jake cleared his throat. He leant on Jamie's shoulder and gave me a bashful smile, threatening to liquidize my legs. "I know you just met us all, and I know it's late, but we'd really like for you to come with us."

I exhaled a little too loudly. "With you? With you where?"

"Just to hang out for a bit, chat some more. I know I unloaded a lot on you all at once. I'd love to talk it over more with you and explain things properly because there aren't many of us. Empaths need to stick together. We're stronger together. That's why we have our team."

Hang out and chat. I could do that. I had to. This was really happening, my impossible dreams coming true, and I had to find out more. I couldn't let them just leave me in my normal life again after this. My parents weren't expecting me home now and I doubted I'd be missed at the shelter. I could spend all night with them if I wanted. And I wanted.

I knew I should be thinking about this more seriously, but I had trouble focusing on anything other than Jake's smile, and the desire to jump in the car with them proved overwhelming. "Sure. Let's go."

Jake and Emma beamed. Jamie's smirk remained in place.

Donny didn't show much expression. His face remained still, like the carving of a god. He checked his watch, also expensive. "We're meant to be flying back tonight."

"We can chat in a café at the airport then until we fly out." Jake looked down at me, his eyelids half closed and small, pouting smile on his lips. "Come with us."

A rush of warmth flooded me. I felt so secure, so sure. I nodded to him.

Looking past their attractive forms was difficult, but in their emotions all I read was excitement and pleasure at finding me. They wanted me. I was special. Like them? Maybe not quite, but they wanted me anyway. Jake and his friends didn't feel like strangers at all. They already felt like family, as if I knew them. I trusted them and going with this group, this team, was the only thing in the world I knew I wanted. It could be my only chance to live my dreams. Mom would tell me to go for it.

Somehow we went from chatting in the rental car, to chatting in the airport, to chatting on the plane.

It wasn't the first time I told my parents I'd be in one place but went somewhere else. But it was the first time that going somewhere else involved a first class flight.

First class was wow. Everyone treated our group like royalty. They squeezed me onto the flight at late notice. Even with strict airport security we breezed through with the team's excess baggage, no questions asked. Jake reassured me we weren't going far, and they would fly or drive me back home any time I wanted. They only flew up to get to the quake site fast, and were only a few hours' drive away from my home town.

If the flight was decadent, their house was something from a fairy tale. Not a house. An abso-frikkin-amaze-balls mansion. Not too old fashioned, not too modern. Perfectly classy. *I wonder which one of them has the trust fund. Probably all of them.*

At first sight of the mansion all I could do was splutter like I'd spontaneously learned another language. "Ung, thas, wha?"

This was luxury on a level I'd never imagined. No, that's not true. It was luxury on the level I daydreamed about every day but never dared think I'd achieve. I'd fallen in with a group of super-powered superstars and felt more than a little afraid at how I was meant to fit in.

"Does anyone else live here?" I asked, when English returned to me.

"Just us. Service staff come and go. A cleaner and a gardener. Oh, and a cook, of course." Jake pulled his car up at the front steps and we all unloaded. His gorgeous wheels looked right at home parked out the front of this place.

"Of course," I whispered.

Jake threw a duffle bag over his shoulder from the trunk of the car and made an "after you" gesture with his other hand.

I took a tentative step toward the wide front doors. Emma grabbed my hand and dragged me at a run. "You're going to have the room next to mine. Come on, I'll show you around."

Emma's tour was informal at best. She dragged me fast-paced down wide halls that mostly looked the same to me, with walls painted stark white and full height windows showing a view of the sea.

"Garage is downstairs that way. Living rooms and all the general stuff through there, but there's a second lounge area back that-away. Kitchen is round there, it's near my room, so that means it will be near your room! The boys' rooms are all off down that hall in the other wing." She pointed in vague directions.

Even if she'd stopped and showed me each one I'm sure I'd get lost in here anyway.

"Whose place is this?" I asked.

"It's a serviced rental. We kind of move around a lot. I think Jake's planning another move soon, or was before we picked you up. I hope we get to stay here a bit longer now. This is our best place yet."

"It must be so nice, travelling around, going on adventures, helping people," I said, then cringed and smiled bashfully at Emma. "So that sounded lame, but I won't lie, you guys are my new idols. How did you all get together?"

Emma twirled and started walking backward to look at me while she talked. "Jake and Jamie are brothers of course. I guess the 'path thing runs in families sometimes, or whatever causes it can hit siblings or people growing up closely together. We don't really know what it's all about. We just know we have it and it's cool." Emma grinned. "So anyway, Jake and Jamie found Donny first. None of us knows much about Donny, he keeps pretty quiet. I do know they were all surprised to find each other. That's when they realized there really were other people like them out there, and made more of an effort to look. Wasn't long after that they found me. At a funeral, would you believe it?"

I wasn't sure what to say, wondering who might have died, and Emma kept smiling, despite the flash of grief and guilt coming from her.

"Then it's been, like, forever, with just us. I've been wishing for another girl on the team. And here we are, ta-da!"

Emma swung a door open and gave me a nudge into the room with her hip. "Nice?"

Not nice. Incredible. King sized modern four-poster bed. Wide screen wall mounted television. Doors to what I imagined were a walk-in-robe and ensuite. Wide bay windows. Ocean view. *Balcony.* I panted a little.

"I know, right? I told you you'd love it here. I called ahead and got Ms. Penny to set the room up for you while she was cleaning. You probably want a shower after being up all night. I know I do. There'll be towels in the bathroom, you can borrow shampoo and stuff from my bathroom next door. Help yourself to whatever you like."

Emma opened the door and showed me the ensuite. The other door was a walk-in closet, empty except for a bathrobe and slippers. I was suddenly conscious that I only had one set of clothes. I compared my average, straight up and down figure to Emma, who was tall and impossibly curvy for her slim frame. I doubted she'd have much to fit me, let alone suit me.

"I didn't pack," I muttered, dazed. I didn't do anything other than get on a plane without planning. I sat down hard on the bed. *What was I doing? I didn't think things through very well.* My skin turned clammy.

"Honey, we'll buy you whatever you need. You're special, like us, you can have whatever you want. And now I have a girl to go shopping with! We are going to buy you so much stuff." Emma came and sat next to me. She put her arm over my shoulder and squeezed. "You okay? Oh, you're probably coming down from the buzz. That would have been your first major use of the powers, right?"

"Is this what happens? I feel like I don't know anything yet. Do I need training or something?" I flopped back onto the bed, my feet still dangling over the edge.

"We don't really do the training thing. More learn on the job. It's mostly natural anyway, we figure."

"So it just happens? Or do I need to make it happen?"

Emma lay back on the bed as well, propped up on one elbow. Her hair fell around her like a curtain and smelled of raspberries. "A bit of both. Some of the power kicks in naturally, but you can focus to absorb even more. It's like when someone is feeling a strong emotion, it sort of floods out of them. Like the human mind - or heart, I don't know - can't hold so much feeling inside." She made her hand into a fist and placed it on her chest. "Ever felt like that, like your emotions are more than you can stand? It's that excess we can tap into. I mean, emotions are powerful, right?"

I put a hand on my own chest, mirroring her. "When those looters came at me, I managed to protect myself, sort of. They were so angry and it was like their energy rushed into me, and I moved faster than I thought I could. And I should have bruises, but I don't."

Emma shifted down onto her back as well and punched her hands at the air above her. "It's bad ass, right? Hate sets up our bodies for defense and healing, excitement gives us energy. Fear speeds us up. There's obviously a lot of overlap with emotions so it all gets a bit fuzzy."

"What about other emotions? Sadness?"

"Ick. Avoid sad people, despair is just useless." Emma stuck her tongue out like she'd tasted something off.

"Love?"

"Aw, you're cute! I wouldn't go holding out to experience tapping into true love if I were you. Lust is where the power's at." She winked at me and I blushed.

Emma's pocket started pinging and she tugged out her phone from the skin-tight denim. "It's Jake. Ooh, another job already?"

Wow. This place is so big they text each other inside.

"Come on, let's go get the info."

She grabbed me by the hand and we were off again. I was caught up in a red-headed whirlwind and her enthusiasm was contagious. I found myself giggling at how lost I was when we reached a room where the guys waited.

Everyone except Emma and me had showered and changed. It made me self-conscious of the scent of overnight-flight I wore. Jake had changed into a tight black tee under a leather motorbike jacket. I barely noticed the other two guys who stood either side of him. It was as though their hotness just enhanced Jake's. Back-up singers to the lead vocal talent.

He smiled at me and I felt like I was in the right place again.

"What is it?" Emma bent at the knees and sprang up again like an excited child.

"I'll tell you on the way. We have to leave right now if we're going to get anything done. Livvy, I'm sorry to do this to you but we really can't miss this one. I'd bring you along, but it's too dangerous for someone so fresh."

My inner voice whined like a little puppy being left home alone. I didn't understand why they couldn't even tell me where they were going or what they were doing. Paranoia scratched at the corner of my brain. Jake patted me on the shoulder and all my worries floated away. *Don't be selfish, Livvy, they've just got important hero stuff to do.* "Yeah, I can understand. Umm… What should I do?"

"Get settled in, cleaned up. Ms. Penny left after her morning rounds but Sophie, our cook, is in so feel free to call the kitchen for whatever you need and she'll help you out." Jake pointed at an intercom near the door. I had seen one like it in my room too, but I didn't know what it was at the time.

"Take a car into town if you like, or just hang here. We've got all the channels," Jamie added, and they headed to the door and down the hall.

Emma popped her head back in. "I'll take you shopping tomorrow, I promise!"

I nodded and remained planted in the room as I heard their footsteps fade. My first move was to inspect the intercom, and press the button labeled "Kitchen".

A husky woman's voice buzzed out of the box. "This is Sophie."

I paused, embarrassed.

"Is this Livvy? Hi, love, what can I do for you?"

"I think I'm lost."

Sophie managed to find me from my description of the room in which I had been left, and gave me a slightly more formal tour than Emma's. The house layout was actually well structured and not nearly as daunting as I first believed. She made me a range of cute snacks that looked like they were from a fancy restaurant and left me to explore.

I felt like an intruder here without the team. It was so good spending last night with them all. A bond had formed, as if I really belonged. A secure contentedness that made me glow and want to stay with them forever. Now I was on my own, hours from home, I kept feeling confused, concerned about how I'd gotten here and what I'd left behind. Like a pair of uninformed parents, and my phone charger. My phone lay lifeless on the bed.

The day was getting on and I worried I'd been discovered missing by now. Even if Trevor assumed I went home, or my parents assumed I stayed longer at the shelter, sooner or later one would contact the other and there would be trouble. *What was I thinking? My parents must be freaking out.*

I attempted to turn on my phone, hoping for a last scrap of power, but it didn't respond. This palace seemed to be designed only for room-to-room communication, and the landline out didn't work. And with Jake off who knows where, getting home again was off the cards as well, for now.

I filled my stomach, took a shower and put my dirty clothes back on, feeling apprehensive and... well, just grouchy. To fill the time until the team returned, I decided to find the garage.

I never found it. Instead I stumbled across the prestige car show room. When Jamie said to take a car, I didn't realize what sort of selection he meant. They had six cars between them, each of which probably cost as much as six ordinary cars, or, you know, a house. I barely recognized the badges, except ones like Maserati I only knew from TV shows about rich people.

I buzzed Sophie in the kitchen again and told her I'd be going for a walk. I didn't have a driver's license yet - thanks again to my family's no-car policy

- and even if I did, the stress of even scratching up one of these cars could turn me prematurely gray. But I did want to get out of this place. The big building left me at a loss without the others around, and I was never very keen on watching TV. On screen, I saw changes in the faces of the actors, but they lacked energy or the connection I felt in real life.

I figured I'd head into town and kill time at a cinema. While TV left me cold, I always loved going to the movies. I guess I understood why now. My Empath abilities couldn't pick up emotions across a small screen, but they could pick up the vibe of a room of people sitting in the dark, all feeling the same thing.

Sophie asked if I'd be needing dinner. I still had twenty bucks cash on me, so I said I'd find something while I was out. I hoped I'd also find a pay phone. She gave me the visitor's security code for the keypad entry to get back in and I headed off.

The mansion was at the top of a hill and a long winding road lead down into town, past a few other mansion-like estates perched on the rocky cliff-side, overlooking the sea. A breeze from the ocean pushed at my back.

Sophie had given me directions to the cinema and it proved easy to find. I bought my ticket but was disappointed when I went in and was the only person there. It proved more depressing than watching TV. By the time the movie was over it had grown dark, and so had my mood. I found myself wandering aimlessly through the unfamiliar town, trying to get my thoughts in order. I questioned how long I'd been wandering but had no way to check the time. I'd made my way into a poorer area, where every second storefront was boarded up and layered in crude graffiti.

Despite the lofty elite on the hillside, the town looked like it had seen better days. It made my home town look downright posh with its little boutique shops like Mom's.

Mom.

I swallowed hard. Mom and Dad must be frantic by now. I hadn't found a pay phone that still worked, and dreaded making the call even if I did. I had no idea what I'd tell them.

I tried not to beat myself up so much. I'd just had some life changing events take place. I was fine, and I'd let them know as soon as I could.

What would they think if I never went back home? I would have been off to college in a year anyway. Now I didn't even know if I was going back to school. I had no idea what was ahead of me, but it wasn't as though college had an Empath 101 course I could take. Shaking my head, I decided I needed to stick with Jake and the team. Somehow, I trusted Jake. One way or another, he'd look after me.

While trying to justify my actions, a sound caught my attention. A range of noises reminding me all too clearly of my confrontation with the looters - taunting, laughing, the sounds of anger and hard objects thudding against flesh. It came from a side street up ahead.

If someone was in trouble, maybe I could do something. I could use my powers, now I knew what they were. I wasn't the old me anymore. Now, I was superhero princess me. Awesome Olivia was here to help.

I approached the side street carefully, going over the pros and cons in my head. No chance to call the cops this time. My flat phone had been left back in my room. If I did this, I'd have to do it with caution. I'd have to be clever. Jake hadn't mentioned secret identities yet and I didn't see the other guys wearing costumes, but I assumed it was best not to flaunt my powers. I also didn't really want to tear off someone's hand.

Peeking around the corner, I saw two guys beating on a third. They had him pressed to a wall, taking turns slugging him in the stomach. They called him names - homo, trailer trash - just like high school but with more violence. The guy they beat didn't struggle and I worried they'd already gone too far. I tried to tap their emotions, get some strength, speed, something I could use.

A cold emptiness crept over me instead. Maybe I wasn't close enough? *Damn it, how did this work?* Their victim didn't look well. I had to do something fast.

Stepping into the alley, I took a position hidden in shadows and yelled. "Police. Stop what you're doing."

All three jumped at my voice, and the emptiness cleared. A wave of anger, excitement and fear flowed off the attackers and I felt power build inside me. *Oh yes, I could do this.*

The two holding the third guy down blocked most of my view of him, but they all seemed about my age. The pair of bullies wore beanies, one blue, one red, probably sports teams but what would I know. My family was more likely to attend an art gallery crawl than watch sports. They muttered between themselves then one of them called out. "You're no cop. Just get gone. You see nothing here."

I flexed an arm, feeling the strength in it. Part of me wanted to use it, but I tried to stay smart. The power was my safety net only. "Come on guys, just leave him alone. I'm not going anywhere, and I don't think you want a witness here."

The beanie twins did that chin lift thing guys do when communicating without words. One kept a hold of their prey and the other stalked toward me. I took a step back out onto the main street to see if there was anyone else around, but it was empty. So I stepped forward and me and blue-beanie-boy squared off. Up close I could see he twitched and swayed slightly. He had a badly grown goatee and stunk of alcohol.

"She's just some skinny chick!" he called back to his mate. He laughed and turned away, telling me to go. He talked fast and every second word he spat was a swear word. I hated when people talked like that. No class.

He headed back to his friend and I followed at his heels.

"I'm not going to let you keep beating that guy."

"Don't." The grunt of opposition came from the guy against the wall. He slouched, as though he'd fall if red-beanie-boy's hand on his shoulder didn't pin him to the wall. Stringy hair fell over his face. His effort to talk earned him another fist in the stomach.

"See, no one wants you around." Blue-beanie-boy spun back at me and thrust out an arm to push me away. I sidestepped easily and he lost balance, diving forward after his arm and landing hard on the pavement.

As he hit the ground I felt the force of his anger burst around him, accompanied by his loud swearing. I made an effort to absorb it all, like soaking in sunshine through my skin. I felt my body respond, every cell working at perfect efficiency.

He pushed himself back off the ground and dusted himself off. "You're going to get it!"

He came at me swinging.

I maneuvered around a street sign and his fist cracked on the metal instead. More swearing. I had no problem keeping away from him, drunk and uncoordinated as he was, but I was only making him angrier. I wanted them to back off and leave without having to hurt anyone. Brilliantly, all I'd done was prove for a second time that one girl on her own wasn't enough to scare off angry guys.

After another bout of swearing, his friend let his victim go and came to join in. He didn't stumble around like drunken blue-beanie. Backed into a wall, I lifted my fists to start fighting back.

Down the street, a siren wailed. Perfect timing.

I shrugged innocently. "Did I forget to mention I already called the cops? Time to run, kiddies."

Their emotions changed to fear, and they finally took my advice, bolting off into the night.

I took a few deep breaths and the siren passed by, revealing the red of a fire truck down the other end of the alley way.

I just saved someone. All on my own. I let out a whoop and punched the air, grinning like a fool.

The guy they'd left beaten had slumped down against the wall, his knees against his chest. He seemed to be catching his breath as well.

I held out my hand to help the guy up. "Are you okay?"

He ignored me and pushed himself up to his feet against the wall. A breath hissed out through his clenched teeth. "What were you doing? You should have left. You could have gotten hurt."

I froze with my hand still outstretched and my smile slipped. Not exactly the response I expected. "I was just trying to help."

He turned and faced me fully. Average build, baggy clothing, dusty brown hair, pasty skin, nothing special at all. But his eyes transfixed me. Gray like wet concrete, they held me like a trap and the coldness I felt earlier crept back in.

"I didn't need your help. This happens all the time."

"A playful rumble, huh? What if they went too far this time?"

He just shrugged like he didn't even care. He winced at each small movement of his torso, even talking. I could tell he was in pain but otherwise his face was blank and I couldn't read a single emotion from him. It irritated me more than his criticisms of my rescue effort.

"You would have been messed up if you weren't lucky."

"I wasn't lucky, I was... clever, and I saved you!" I found myself yelling. I couldn't read him at all. *Why wasn't he happy? Why was he treating me like this?*

Blood dripped from his nose onto his light gray t-shirt. He zipped his jacket up over it and pulled the hood over his head. "Whatever."

He walked away.

All energy drained from me. I spent my last cash to get a taxi back up to the mansion. I found it empty. Confused and alone, I crawled into bed.

I couldn't sleep. Gray eyes kept haunting me. Stupid, unappreciative eyes.

PART TWO

ANGEL MASKS

Jake and the team returned mid-morning. Seeing him again knocked my dull mood away. It also felt better having clean clothes. Ms. Penny had washed and dried what I'd been wearing while I had breakfast in bed in a robe and slippers. Pretty people and decadence took the edge off real quick.

We all sat in a lounge room. I wasn't sure which one or what its exact designation was. The white leather couches were immaculate and the rug so dense and fluffy I almost wanted to sit on it more than the couch. The guys relaxed from whatever their secret overnight mission had been.

I had to deal with contacting my parents. I felt lame bringing it up to the group and I doubted my parents would be very happy either. I mustered up the will to speak. Jake smiled at me and I almost lost it.

Concentrating on something other than his perfect features proved difficult.

"Is there a way I can get my phone charged? I want to call my parents."

Jake sat next to me with his feet up on the glass coffee table and head back. He straightened up to look at the flat phone I exhibited in my hand.

"Don't worry about it. We'll get you a new phone. Ems, you taking our new girl out shopping today?"

Emma had draped herself full length down the opposite couch, leaving Donnie and Jamie in designer shaped armchairs, which looked more fancy than comfortable. At least for guys of their size.

Emma moaned and pouted, lifting her head with exaggerated effort. "Yeah, sure. I could probably stay awake for shopping."

"I still need to call my parents. Ms. Penny said the landline isn't connected here, so maybe, could I borrow someone's phone, to let them know where I am?"

The longer this waited, the more the knot in my stomach tightened. *What could my parents be thinking of me? They probably thought I was buried under a collapsed building somewhere.*

Jake shuffled across the lounge and put his arm around my shoulders.

The knot vanished. A warm glow replaced it and I tried not to purr.

"You're worried about your folks, about them worrying about you? I forget sometimes, since me and Jamie have been on our own for so long. Do you want me to take you home?"

He sounded so disappointed. Yesterday I might have said yes, but not now they were all back here with me. I didn't want to be anywhere else. "Oh, no, I can just call them. I'm sure they'll be angry, but I need-"

Jake gave my shoulders a squeeze. "Do you want me to sort it out for you? Look, I'm great with parents, and it's always better to deal with things face to face, right? I've got to head back to your town tomorrow anyway, so I'll stop by and smooth things over. Save you from bearing the parental brunt."

I tilted my head and winced, working up to say no, which was hard. But seriously, my parents could have called me in as a missing person by now.

Jake took my chin in his hand, leaning so close I almost thought he was going to kiss me. "Let me do this for you."

I exhaled over wobbly lips. I smiled and gave my okay. My parents could wait another day if it meant getting an in-person explanation instead of dodgy phone call, and I just knew Jake could make them understand. He made everything better just by being there.

I started to offer to go with him, to see my parents and to spend time alone with Jake, but Donnie interrupted in his deep, dry voice.

"Livvy, we want you right here this week so at first sign of an event nearby we can take you with us. It's time to get to know you better and see how your powers manage."

Emma sat up with far more energy than she'd shown before. "Then you can be part of the team for real!"

I glowed, and wondered if it was visible to them all.

"What do you want me to tell your folks?" Jake asked.

I thought for a moment. "Tell them I'm following my dreams."

Emma did take me shopping that afternoon, but we didn't get a new phone. We mostly bought new clothes for Emma. She held nothing back, snapping up every designer item taking her fancy, paying cash for everything. She tried to encourage me to do the same, but I only managed to humbly request a new pair of jeans, two tops, some PJs and underwear sets. At least I had some clothes to change into now. Soon

I'd feel more comfortable taking what I wanted like Emma did. Soon, I'd be part of the team for real.

During the week each of the team members ducked out individually for this or that. They weren't much for explaining what they were doing or where they were going, and I didn't want to seem naggy with questions. Maybe they had day jobs? I somehow doubted it, unless it was just cover for secret identities. No way did they need the money. No one did any Empath power training, which disappointed me. They didn't even seem as interested in it as I did. The only training done was daily body sculpting work-outs. I joined in and they encouraged me even though I was pathetic.

Jake returned with a new phone for me, already programmed with the team's numbers, and a report on my parents.

"They were worried, of course, but my top notch Empath skills had them feeling better in no time. Here, check this out." Jake pulled out his phone and showed me a ten second video of him sitting on my couch with my parents, all three smiling and waving. "I told them we're friends from school, that we picked you up and let you stay at ours instead of the shelter. Made a few other excuses about flat phones, extra volunteer work together, yadda yadda, and they're happy to let you stay with us as long as you like."

I wondered if forever was included. I needed to go back home myself for visits sometime soon, and reminded myself to give my parents super-hugs for letting me do this. I knew Mom would understand. Mom ran away from a backwater slum when she was fourteen and lived on her own for years, waitressing in cafes during the days and working nights and weekends building her own business. She met the man of her dreams and now ran her own shop. My mom was amazing and always encouraged me to follow my dreams too.

I thanked Jake for the new phone, and tried it out by taking a photo of us together. I spent most of my free hours for the rest of the week staring at that photo.

On Sunday night, Donnie and Jamie called in from the industrial district across the city. A warehouse had gone up in flames, and they said it looked like a good first event for me.

It was time for me to prove myself, although a burning building intimidated me. I'd never witnessed a real fire before. What was I expected to do? I felt too embarrassed to ask and appear dumb to the others.

This was my chance to see what I could really do. Maybe save someone's life.

Jake drove the Maserati there faster than I thought was safe. Emma took the front seat and I squeezed into the pocket sized back with Emma's reasoning that I had the shortest legs. Maybe Jake sensed my anxiety, and explained the situation more as we stopped down the road from the pillar of black smoke marking the fire.

"Don't stress. There's no one in the buildings, the whole industrial park has been evacuated. Nothing but stock and structures at risk." Ever the gentleman, he popped his front seat forward and helped extract me from the back of the two-door sports car.

I noticed Donnie's black jeep parked a little further down the street, and he and Jamie loaded something into the trunk. We wandered down to meet them.

"So, what will I be doing?" I tried to sound brave.

Jake nodded to the other guys before coming back to my question. "Just watching. The fire fighters are working hard to get the fire under control before it spreads. There's some serious adrenaline and emotion involved in that, so just feel out the situation and see what you can use."

We were still a building or two away and I already felt warmth. I wondered if it was from the fire or the emotions of those fighting it. We ducked through a hole in a chain link fence to get close and observe from somewhere hidden so the officials wouldn't send us away.

"What would you guys normally be doing, if I weren't learning?"

"For a fire? Not really a lot we can do. If someone was inside I'd rush in for the save, but Empath powers don't really make us more effective at putting out flames." Jake smiled and winked. I wondered if I could rush into a burning building to save someone. Mouthing off at punks seemed altogether different. But I wanted to be someone who would do that.

The two story warehouse glowed like a jack-o'-lantern. I stared in awe at such destructive, beautiful power. Flames painted the walls and the heat scorched and dried my unprotected skin even from this distance. The smell was off, like bad eggs and car burn outs. Fortunately, most of the smoke blew the other way.

We watched the fire fighters doing their thing, calling orders back and forth, dragging hoses, working pumps on the truck. All knew their roles. They worked as a team. I'd be part of a team like that soon, but even better. I looked sidelong at Jake, his hair and skin glowing golden in the fire light. *Part of his team.*

Excess emotions flowed off the fire fighters and I made myself a magnet, letting power soak in through my pores.

Jake bumped my shoulder with his. "How are you feeling? Got the mojo yet?"

"Yeah, feeling good. Awesome even."

Jake held up his palm flat in front of me. "Give me your best shot."

"Really?"

Jake rolled his eyes. "And don't be holding back. We don't take wimps."

I raised an eyebrow and lifted my fist to the challenge. I could feel muscles tense and coil. The sensation and awareness, the pure power, made me feel drunk. I smacked my fist into his palm.

Jake whistled, dramatically shaking off the hurt. "Nice, some real potential there. How about a race?"

My imagination went on its own race into the future, Jake and me running through the deserted warehouses, giggling, speeding after each other, tumbling into a heap, our lips so close and then…

Something caught my eye over at the fire. My sight had improved as well, the way it had the night after I volunteered. A sheet of corrugated iron peeled itself off the roof, lifting under the hot gusts from the fire like a strange kite. It lingered in the air then fell in a deadly dive bomb straight at one of the fire fighters.

I didn't have to question anymore if I'd run to save someone. I just ran.

I thought I heard someone cursing behind me as I bolted at the man. I'd never moved so fast. *Was I still visible or just a blur?* I collided with the fire fighter in a tackle and we rolled six feet in a tumble together. The corrugated iron scraped and tore on the concrete where he had been.

The fire fighter looked from me to the jagged, red hot iron with his jaw unhinged. His face softened and I held my breath, waiting for the praise I'd missed with last save I made. Instead I found myself wrenched to my feet and dragged away.

"Idiot! What were you thinking?" Jake hissed as he pulled me along. We moved fast and were back at the car before I knew it. "We can't be seen here. You can't be seen doing things like that. People will start asking questions."

I stuttered and dropped my head, screwing my face up to stop myself crying. He might as well have slapped me. "I didn't do good?"

"It's important we all keep a low profile. You're not going to be trouble for us? Trying to be a big hero?" Jake's eyes had turned stony.

"No, I- I just wanted to help him. I'm sorry. I get we have to do things carefully."

Emma, Jamie and Donnie caught up. I could tell they were all irritated, or downright angry.

Jake softened and my world turned right again. "It's okay. It's easy to get caught up in the powers sometimes. You did a good thing. Just remember, if you're going to be part of the team, you have to learn to take orders."

I nodded, relieved as the team's anger at me lessened. "Of course. I can do that. I want to be part of the team, more than anything."

No one talked on the drive home. I kept busy berating myself internally. *I have to be smarter or they won't accept me. I should have known I wasn't special enough as is to get an easy "A" on their Empath tests.*

Those thoughts mixed with the thrill I relived of saving the fireman's life. Even if it was wrong to expose myself or my powers, I felt like I'd done the right thing. Jake was probably just angry I got there first. Would the fireman have thanked me?

Of course he would have. Only emotionless gray-eyed robot types don't thank people.

Once those eyes came into my head, I couldn't wipe them away again for the rest of the night.

I woke up the next morning to Emma bouncing on the side of my bed. She giggled at my shock and headed back out the door, calling over her shoulder.

"Come on, wake up. Make yourself pretty and meet us in the formal lounge. We'll be waiting."

Ominous? Or maybe... I rushed through a shower and put on my best choice of limited clothing. I tried three options for my hair then left it out long, running a straightener over just the front to tidy it up.

I tried two lounge rooms before I found the formal one where everyone waited. I wasn't sure I'd been in this one before. A massive gilt-framed mirror dominated one wall, and everyone sat in armchairs around a stool in front of it.

Emma stood up, squealing. "It's makeover time!"

She ushered me onto the stool and I sat awkwardly. "Makeover?"

Jake leant forward in his armchair and smirked, his wide shoulders on display in a fitted shirt. "We want you on the team, Livvy. So we need you to be the best you can be."

Okay, makeover. Fun. Just like on reality shows. I could go a fancy new hair style for sure. The prospect of dying it something other than brown got me smiling. I was getting the princess treatment again, which was nice. I had worried I'd blown it last night with my hero stunt. Jake didn't seem angry anymore, but eyed me critically, running a hand through his golden hair and rubbing his chiseled chin. I tried to sit tall and not be overwhelmed with self-consciousness.

Emma circled me and played with my hair. "You're already so pretty, there won't be too much work to do. Just a few things to really make you pop."

I burned with a blush. People told me I was pretty before, but I figured I was average-pretty at best. And *pretty* isn't *amazing. It would be nice to be amazing like everyone else in this room.*

"If you have suggestions for my hair, I'm up for anything." I poked my loose hair to highlight my fashion cluelessness.

"We'll do the hair for sure, and much more. Don't worry, any work you have done is on us." Emma grinned.

Hang on, what? "Work done?" I asked.

Jamie spoke up. "She should get her lips and tits filled."

I laughed out loud but no one else did.

My laughter shut off fast. "Oh. I thought you were joking."

Jake cut in with a soft tone. "Sorry, Jamie can be a bit crass. Don't worry, it wouldn't be extreme. Not as much as Emma's had done. It wouldn't suit your frame."

Emma folded her arms under her abundant bust to demonstrate.

"She could also have the bridge of her nose taken down a little, and narrowed at the base."

Jake nodded. "You're right, Donnie. Always with the eye for detail."

I wanted to hide. *Are they seriously talking about plastic surgery? They're pranking, they must be. Just pushing it to see how long they can keep me going.*

At least Jake wasn't being as critical as the others. Famous last words.

"She needs to get some mouth work done too. The crooked front teeth have to go," Jake said.

I felt something shatter inside me. There was no joke here. My mouth fell open as the concept settled in. *They expect me to get plastic surgery to be part of the team. And dental work.* I closed my mouth. Did I really think someone like Jake could be attracted to me as is? Maybe not, but I hoped. I hoped he saw beyond the brown-haired, brown-eyed, average-pretty to something special inside. That was my dream. Not him wanting to change me with plastic surgery.

"Honey, don't feel bad! It's not like it's just you. We've all had work done." Emma hugged me around the shoulders then pounced back into an empty armchair. "We're talking about way less for you than I had. But then, I wanted a lot of it myself."

All of them? Even the guys? "Why?"

"To be this fab-u-lous," Emma drawled, posing like a model in her chair.

Jake tilted his head and gave me a kind smile. It helped settle my nerves better than hot chocolate. His smile made everything better and I started wondering if I could get plastic surgery, for him, if it would keep him near me, so I could always feel this warm and safe. "We all do it because it helps with our powers. Same with keeping ourselves in good shape. It pays off to be attractive."

"I told you. Lust is where the power is at," Emma said.

I frowned. "I don't understand."

Donnie's voice was dryer than usual. He spoke slowly, like trying to wake a sleep walker, or talking to someone really dumb. "When people are physically attracted to us, we receive power from that emotion. It means we can get them to do what we want. Anything we suggest is accepted easily, a bit like hypnotism. The more attracted they are, the better it works. So we make ourselves physically desirable. Did you really think we were all born this perfect?"

Emma chimed in. "Haven't you ever had it easy picking up guys and getting them to do whatever you want? Buy you drinks, give you their number, give you their whole damn wallet?"

Not really. There had never been anyone I was interested enough in to try picking up. I was waiting for my prince, my Jake. Sure, there had been a couple of guys who hit on me before but I never thought that I could use that to my advantage. Just how open to suggestion did the lust power make people?

The air rushed out of me so quickly I felt faint. *Would it make someone open to the suggestion of leaving home with a group of strangers in the middle of the night?*

Everything started to spiral and I stared at the floor, trying to take steady breaths. I should have asked more questions. I should have gone home and thought about what I was doing. I should have told my parents. Any sane person would have done those things. I liked to think I was sane, but I also didn't like the idea that Jake used his powers on me.

I looked up to ask something, anything to get reassurance his power hadn't been used on me. Jake smiled. His perfect smile. My concerns fell away like sand under a wave. In the past, that wave buoyed me and left me floating blissfully, but now the water was cold, leaving me feeling numb and confused. Was it happening again? I could hardly tell my own desires and emotions over what I was being told I should do. *I do want this. I'm following my dream.* Maybe plastic surgery didn't fit into my dream but I hadn't ever been really clear on what my dreams were anyway.

"So, my lovely Livvy, the question is - what are you willing to do to be part of the team? If you can't even handle some plastic surgery..."

The thought of my chance to be part of the team slipping away made me feel panicky. I didn't think I could cope with going home, being normal again after seeing how Jake and the others lived. The way I felt after saving the guy in the alley, after saving the fireman, maybe that was the dream I should be chasing. If I wanted to be a hero, to be exceptional, my best chance to do that was with these people, unlike anyone I'd ever met before.

"Anything, I'll do anything."

I moped up and down the shopping mall, arms loaded with fancy paper bags from deluxe boutiques. I should have felt like a star, out on a spending spree with a fat wad of someone else's cash, but all I could think about was buying the right things to make myself look better. I didn't know what I was doing and wished Emma was here to guide me, but she went off on some important lunch date. She had great fashion sense and wore everything so well. Or was that the plastic surgery? Just how much did she have done to look so fantastic? I wondered how she looked before.

Jake said he wouldn't rush me into anything major, it was all just something to think about for now. They wanted me on the team and seemed happy I was willing to do what I needed to be with them. Jake told me there were so few people like us. Maybe he felt they couldn't leave me out. But I had to step up and be valuable to the group. *Maybe I can do it without going under the knife.* My shopping choices better be amazing in that case.

Whether it was my thoughts or the swag weighing me down, I felt exhausted. I needed fuel, and stepped out of the mall onto the street to find a coffee shop.

That's when I saw him again. He sat across the street in a park, eyes down, reading, but I didn't need to see them to know their exact shade of gray.

I felt bad that I'd yelled at him. Sure I'd saved him from further beating, and that was a point to me, but yelling at the victim wasn't very heroic behavior. I decided to apologize and see how he was recovering. Now we were in a less stressed environment, maybe he'd also say thank you, which I had to admit I really wanted. I needed reassurance to know I did the right thing, since "the right thing" was starting to get very fuzzy in my mind. I took a deep breath to build up some courage and marched across the road.

Few people were in the park, and if they were they rushed through rather than linger in the neglected property. A wooden play fort dominated the central area, the kind which wouldn't get built these days for being too dangerous to kids, but was the kind kids loved. I saw one boy look longingly its direction before being dragged the other way by his dad. The lawn throughout was uneven, spotted with dandelions and longer than it should be. I shuffled through it to the bench where the guy I'd saved sat.

I stood still in front of him and he didn't move. Ignoring me, or absorbed in the dog-eared paperback, I couldn't tell. The same weird, cold, emptiness I felt when I first saw him crept into my bones. I cleared my throat and he looked up.

He looked better in the daylight, less pasty and more ivory skinned. I spaced out for a moment wondering how my olive skin would look pressed against it. *Where did that come from?*

"Hi?" He sounded confused. There was a slight rosiness to his cheeks and under his eyes, almost like he'd been crying, but I couldn't get an emotional read.

"Do you remember, the other night? I was, uh, the alley, and those guys, and, uh, I'm Livvy." My inability to sense any hint of emotion from this guy threw me. It was just like watching TV. I saw the movement and angles of his face and body but couldn't sense anything real. Almost as though he wasn't even really there.

He nodded slowly and a tiny smile emerged. Or maybe it was a nervous tic. I couldn't tell either way with this blank slate. Even Donnie showed mountains of emotion in comparison.

"I remember. I'm Dean."

"I was just about to get a coffee. Want to join me?" I thumb-pointed over my shoulder at the coffee bar in front of the mall.

Dean stared at it for a moment, his eyebrows twitching. He closed his book and I saw it was so worn it had no real cover anymore. I wondered what he was reading.

"Sure."

He stood up and I juggled my bags back into carrying order as we crossed the road. I ordered a cappuccino with extra froth and Dean waved off getting anything. We took a booth and my bags piled around me on the bench.

"So..." I struggled to be casual. "Are you feeling okay? Since, you know, I saved you from those guys?"

Dean shrug-nodded but didn't say anything.

The red around Dean's eyes made them look less gray, more the color of worn denim. They had a depth I kept falling into. I couldn't help staring, trying to get some hint of what this guy felt. All I got from him was that same chilling, hollow feeling.

He leaned back in the booth and unzipped his jacket. The baggy shirt underneath was gray and it struck me that he seemed to be wearing the same clothes I saw him in before. Not that they were unique in any way to tell for sure. They were clean, and I smelled plain soap and a smoky musk as he took off his jacket. The stitching had come undone around the collar of the t-shirt and the fabric looked thin.

His hair fell down in front of his face, soft and also clean. Maybe it just looked stringy the other night from sweat. I saw his lips moving.

Distracted, I completely missed what he said. "Uh, sorry, what?"

"I said I was wondering what you wanted to talk to me about. Are you okay? You seem upset. At least, you aren't smiling like a fool like you were after chasing off those guys."

Great. I had no idea what he was feeling and here he was making guesses about me.

I pulled my lips closed tight. "It's just my teeth. They're all crooked. I didn't realize before but now I kind of hate them."

"You're prettier when you smile."

He said it so plainly, like it was nothing. Not praise, not flattery or a shot at getting something from me. He said it just like a fact, like the sky is blue.

Nothing Dean said felt like it had any emotion so I clung to his words for meaning. Like how he said *prettier* and that maybe the "er" meant he thought I was pretty even now when I wasn't smiling. My heart was doing silly maneuvers and I shook my head, looked into my foamy coffee and added another sugar.

"Your teeth give you character. It's cute, the way one crosses over the other a bit at the front-"

I put my hand over my mouth.

"Sorry, I'm saying dumb things. You shouldn't feel bad about them. But you're going to get them fixed anyway, aren't you? I guess you've got the money to do it." Dean eyed the bags surrounding me.

"Oh, the shopping. I kind of came to stay with friends for a while without packing and needed some things. The money isn't mine. It's sort of complicated." I shuffled around on the seat as though it would hide some of the mountain of purchases behind me, suddenly embarrassed by it all.

"What about that necklace, is it really yours? You were wearing it the other night too. Silver, or…?"

"White gold." I wrapped my hand around the heart shaped pendant I had been wearing since the earthquake, covering it from sight. "My parents bought it for me when I got a B on my last tests."

"Shouldn't that be an A?"

"Probably, but B was the best I could do. It's not like I don't try, I just suck at tests." *And my parents are just big softies.* My vision glazed with tears and I realized how much I was missing them. I blinked the wetness away.

Dean rolled his eyes. I didn't have to sense emotions to know the 'poor you' look.

Did he think I was spoiled? Is that what he was getting at? He was all questions and no answers. I wanted desperately to know why his eyes were red, whether he had been crying or not. I wanted to know how he felt about being attacked and how he felt about me saving him, and I couldn't read a thing.

Embarrassment unfurled inside me without warning, coloring my face. I gulped my coffee to hide it.

A beeping noise distracted me and it took a moment to recognize the message tone of my new phone. I apologized and pulled it out of my pocket.

A message from Jake. I smiled at his name, then pulled my lips back over my teeth again.

Coming to pick U up. Meet west mall exit. C U in 15. Team Stuff.

I typed quickly. *Cya soon.*

I slipped the phone away and told Dean I had to be somewhere.

He helped me load my bags up again and thanked me for the coffee, even though he didn't have anything.

I wasn't sure if I'd see Dean again and I was starting to want to. In the whirlwind my life had become, the last twenty minutes had felt like the only time recently when my feet were safely on the ground. *I could ask for his number, but then what?* He didn't seem that interested in me. I should have just said goodbye, but instead I blurted more crazy words.

"You really think my teeth are okay?"

Dean half-smiled and walked away.

Donnie's jeep stopped in front of me where I waited on the curb, balancing my purchases. I threw them all in the back and climbed in next to Emma who shuffled into the middle seat. It was a full house, with Donnie driving, Jamie shotgun, Jake and I in the back with Emma as an unfortunate barrier between us.

"So, team stuff?"

"Last night at the fire we were getting to know the strength of your powers. Today, it's time to prove you're one of us, part of the team." Jake gave me a serious look, with just enough flirty smile to make me swoon. "Today is a fundraising activity."

"Oh, like, charity work?"

Emma barked a high pitch laugh that faded into a giggle. *Charity work is funny?*

"Fundraising for us, for the team," Jake continued. "We're headed to a bank to make a withdrawal. We need to stock up on the spending cash."

Donnie drove us downtown. The glitzy mall area made way for the industrial and housing estate district. I shook my head. *They're just going to the bank? Why did this need to be done as a team?* Unease gurgled in my stomach. My paranoia was growing sharper claws but I still refused to let it scratch down my painted world.

Emma fished around in a massive designer handbag on her lap and threw what looked like a dead animal to Jamie. She grabbed more hair from the bag - wigs - and passed a black one to Jake. She took a blond wig in each hand and dangled them in front of me. “We’re both going to be blond, like sisters. You’re going to look so cute as a blond.”

I took the wig. A buzz of excitement came from everyone else in the car. “We’re not just withdrawing money, are we?” I wasn’t sure I wanted to hear the answer.

“Sure we are. Just not ours,” said Jamie.

“Um…” That was the answer I didn’t want to hear.

Jake sighed, shaking his head. “My little brother and his abundant tact. It’s not a big deal. You’re with us on this, aren’t you, Livvy? We have to do this to stay a team. Do you think we should have normal jobs with our powers? We’re better than that.”

Donnie glanced at me in the rear vision mirror. “Taking on a new team member is expensive too. Where did you think the money you spent today came from?”

Trust fund? Inheritance? Lottery? I guess that was all a bit naïve. Who has any of that? And I just went out and spent their money, however they’d gotten it, like I had every right.

“But, are you really talking about robbing a bank here? That’s all kinds of dangerous, and, well, illegal.” My heart pumped hard and I wasn’t sure what to think. It was all just too surreal. Movie stuff, not just-left-the-mall stuff.

"Honey, it won't be dangerous at all. We have super powers, remember? We're just going to walk in, bat our eyelashes, ask for the money, and walk out with it. We already scoped this bank, and it's old school. No security screens or anything yet." Emma adjusted her wig into place and reached between the front seats to adjust the rear view mirror to preen. She then turned her preening onto Jamie and Jake's wigs, also now in place. They looked so different, their hair now jet black with mature cuts. It made them seem darker, more dangerous, somehow. "My lunch date was with a worker from there who told me all about the place. We would have left it a bit longer, but now's the best time to hit them. It's welfare check day, and the bank tops up its tellers for everyone coming in to cash their checks. Easy pickings."

Jake brushed Emma away and put on dark sunglasses. "You're just going to be lookout for us this time. Until you get some work done we won't have you taking on a teller, just in case."

I breathed out very slowly, letting it puff out my lips. "I don't know if I can do this. Isn't it wrong?"

"No one will get hurt and the bank won't miss a few cash drawers. We're not taking the vault or anything insane. And we'll use the money to help us do more heroic stuff later on. Promise." Jake winked, and I swore I heard Jamie chuckle.

Jake looked me in the eyes and I felt him forcing the sense of trust, warmth and contentedness on me. I pushed it away. It was easier now. I guess with Jake's recent words and actions, I wasn't as attracted to him as I was before. I saw clearly, felt clearly, and the horror of it almost overwhelmed me.

A physical pain crept into my chest and I realized I was scared of Jake. Scared of what I was doing. Terrified of all of them and what they would do if I didn't cooperate.

Jake watched me, waiting for my response. I put the wig on and smiled. I read once just the act of moving your muscles into a smile made you happy and hoped it would be enough to cover my fear. I tried to shut off the part of my brain saying *no, no, no, no, no,* and focused on Jake's smile. It didn't help. That fake smile. How much of him was real at all? Everything felt wrong.

Emma tilted her head at me and giggled. "Donnie, drive around the block a couple of times while I sort out this girl's hair."

Donnie waited with the car down the street and Emma and I walked into the bank first. A reasonably large place, old fashioned like she said, standing in a row of mostly closed businesses in a dying business district. Only a pawn shop, second hand clothing store and tobacco shop were still open nearby. Inside the bank, a musty smell rose from the threadbare carpet, and the wooden counters looked more like something out of an old western movie than a modern bank. Plexiglas dividers had been bolted on top of them, and a ticket machine stood at the front like a welcoming robot, but they were the only parts of the place that didn't feel like they were from the 1950s. Even the customers inside were generally old, mixed in with a few builders and laborers.

We were seriously going to rob a bank. I played through my memories of how I ended up here. So much was a blur, compelled by these perfect people. But I couldn't blame them. I'd made decisions, I had wanted this. Well, maybe not *this*, exactly. I made sure my oversized sunglasses were still in place and tugged downward at my wig as though I could cover all of my face with it. *If I can just get through this, there has to be a way I can back out gracefully from this whole team thing, right? Will Jake just let me go?*

Emma scoped a security guard and went to do her job, flirting with him and keeping him entirely occupied. I just had to take a seat and keep watch. Only the bank was busy and there were no seats left.

Small detail, but I had to breathe through an anxiety attack as I tried to stand casually in the corner.

Jake and Jamie came in not long after us and took numbers. I practically counted the seconds waiting for them to be called to a teller. I considered just flat-out bolting, but knew Donnie was watching the street.

Jake was called, and Jamie a split second after as two tellers cleared. They were middle-aged ladies who I could tell were already swooning at their approach. Maybe this would be easy after all.

I watched with fascination as Jake leaned forward, his lips almost up against the Plexiglas barrier. I saw the attraction oozing from the lady. She probably would have played with her hair if it weren't back in a very tight business-like bun. She kept on talking and giggling with Jake as she pulled a cash bag from the desk and opened the cash drawer, stuffing bills into the bag a wad at a time.

That's when coldness filled me. I hoped it just meant the air-con had kicked in, but this felt familiar.

The teller with Jake froze, and her flirty grin dropped into a frown. She looked at the bag in her hand like she discovered she held a dead fish. I couldn't hear what she said, but her jaw wobbled up and down. I couldn't tell how she was feeling either.

Jake kept working his act but she wouldn't calm down.

Jamie called over to Jake. Trouble there too.

I heard Jake call back, loud enough for me and Emma to hear, "Change of plans."

The teller stood and made to move away, and suddenly Jake had a shiny silver handgun pointed at her.

No, no, no, no, no.

Jamie pulled a gun from his jacket too, waving it at the waiting customers. "Everyone get back against that wall. You know the deal. If nothing stupid happens then nothing stupid happens."

A large man in grease-covered clothing didn't budge. He drawled in a husky voice, "Come now, boys, don't do anything rash."

"Stupid." Jamie dropped his aim and shot the man in the leg. He crumpled, gasping, clutching at the wound, trying to hold in his blood.

I yelped, heart hammering, and Jake shook his head at me, warning me with his expression. Others in the crowd screamed as well, cowering back.

I turned to Emma, just a few steps away from me with the guard. She couldn't be in on this.

How wrong I was. She held a petite pistol in one hand and she relieved the security guard of his weapons with the other.

"Ems?" I hissed.

"Chill, sister," she hissed back. "A little firearm action will get the sheep scared and our powers kicking in again. Then we can get our goods and clear out fast."

But our powers weren't kicking in. I didn't feel anything, not the slightest tingle, only the cold inside. People shuffled toward the wall, mumbling outrage and prayers. I looked over their faces, all of them terrified, except one. His face was blank and gray eyes stared at me, at my heart pendant, at the same clothing he'd seen me in just half an hour before and the blond wig identifying me as not on the level.

Dean.

I looked away, ashamed.

"I'm not getting the vibe!" Jamie yelled at Jake, who was busy getting the teller to keep clearing drawers.

"Swap," Jake called back, and Jamie swung his gun to the teller, taking over.

Jake scanned the room, coming to stand beside me. "You feeling anything?"

"Just… cold." My eyes turned toward Dean automatically, just for a second. Jake's gaze followed mine and he grunted.

"A blocker. We've got a blocker!" Jake yelled to the others.

"Oh shit," Emma spat.

The hostages against the wall cowered. Dean stood motionless and continued to stare right at me.

Jake patted me on the shoulder. "Good pick, lookout. We'd be in trouble if you hadn't spotted him. Nice, you're making yourself valuable."

I didn't want to be valuable like this. I didn't understand much of what was happening and liked even less. "Why? What's a blocker?"

"People who grow up blocking their feelings, locking them down to the extent it breaks something inside them. Then that block extends out. It messes with our powers," Jake grunted and pointed his gun straight at Dean. "Best to deal with them when they show up. I've seen one lock off an Empath's powers for good."

Jake smiled his comforting smile at me. It chilled me more than the blocking coldness coming from Dean. "Once we get rid of him our powers will work again and we can get all this under control."

"Get rid of? What? No!" I stepped in front of Jake to try and talk him out of it. Stupid move, but I didn't realize he was already at the point of pulling the trigger.

Jake tensed and jerked the gun to the side.

The sound blast from the shot left my whole head numb. It took a moment to hear the screams, and feel the burn in my cheek. My over-sized sunglasses hit the floor.

I turned in slow motion and saw an elderly woman falling to the ground. The pool of blood around her made acid rise in my throat. I knew she was dead, just knew it.

Other customers cried and ran. Jake had lost any control of the situation. The people stumbled right over the old woman's body, stampeding toward the door. Emma and Jamie headed for the door as well. I heard sirens in the distance.

Dean dodged between them but didn't make for the exit.

"Run, you idiot, get out of here!" I screamed.

He yelled back, but all I could hear over the screaming was, "death wish".

I felt something hard press my temple.

"Jake?" I whimpered. I wanted to be strong, but it turned out a gun at your head will cause whimpering.

"I should have known you wouldn't work out, but I didn't think you'd screw things up this much!" He yelled at me, so close spittle hit my face. His finger on the trigger tensed.

The gun fired again and I was slammed aside by a body. Dean cried out as he fell past me and hit the floor. Blood bloomed like red flowers through the fabric on his arm.

The coldness faded and I felt some power come to me, like it had when I surprised Dean and his attackers that night. I guessed when he was shocked he wasn't keeping his feelings under such tight rein and his emotional block didn't extend out. I didn't know. I just knew I had to act fast before Jake felt his powers kick in too.

I stumbled from Dean pushing me clear of the gun shot. I regained my balance fast, spinning with the momentum and knocking the gun from Jake's hand. I continued the spin and cracked my elbow against Jake's jaw, making him fall backwards.

I grabbed Dean by the arm, pulling him to his feet, practically threw him over my shoulder, and made a run for it.

PART THREE

STRENGTH TO FALL

I ran down alleys and side streets, avoiding the sounds of sirens and as many passers-by as possible. Dean bounced over my shoulder where I had him slung in a fireman's carry. Blood from his arm ran down onto the crisp white of my peasant blouse, the cutest of three tops I had chosen to wear this morning to be judged by those… *bad guys.*

I hoped the jostling didn't hurt Dean too much. He was still out of it, otherwise I wouldn't be able to keep moving so fast. I had no idea where I was going or what I should do. I only remembered one thing from first aid class that seemed relevant; the DR ABCs. I had to get Dean and myself out of Danger then check his Responsiveness. I had to get us as far away from Jake as I could. Airway, Breathing and CPR… *It better not come to that.*

Dean moaned and coughed and for a split second I felt relieved. Then the coldness sank into me, leaching all my strength. My legs buckled and we both hit the cracked concrete footpath. My knees grazed through denim as Dean's weight on my back crushed me forward.

I tried to roll him off to the side without hurting either of us more. He moved off me, and leaned up against one of the high metal fences enclosing the backyards around us.

His upper arm still oozed blood. He opened those gray eyes and stared at me.

I blushed red all over. I had no idea what he thought of me right now.

"We should get you to a doctor, or a hospital. We have to do something about your arm."

He turned his head to the gunshot wound and brought his other hand up to grasp it and suppress the bleeding. "No. Hate hospitals."

He flinched at his own touch and stared at me again. "I don't understand you."

I coughed a laugh and only a breathy noise came out.

"Were you with them? Or are you just wearing a wig for fun?"

Reaching up, I patted the side of my head, feeling the curling blond waves of the wig. I tugged it off and dropped it on the weed covered pathway.

"It's complicated." I didn't know how to explain without sounding bad, because there wasn't a way. I'd done the wrong thing.

"Complicated. Like your shopping money not really being your money. But you tried to stop them. Why? You have a death wish, taking on people like that?"

"I'm not a criminal. I mean, I didn't want to be. I just got caught up with the wrong people. I thought they were the right ones. I don't know." I glared at the pile of synthetic blond hair on the ground, angry at my own excuses. "I just wanted to be a hero."

"A dead hero by the sounds of it." Dean pushed himself up to his feet and walked away, cradling his arm.

I almost took out my phone but didn't know who to call or where to go next. I sat on the concrete and tugged at the weeds, tearing them out in showers of dirt, taking my pain out on them. Jake had tried to shoot me, kill me. He'd definitely kill Dean if he saw him again. Everything told me if I wasn't with Jake, I was against him. He'd come after me. I couldn't go home, Jake knew where I lived. I'd given him the address. He'd been there, seen my parents, manipulated them.

I had no money left for travel or accommodation and didn't know the area well enough to get myself moving in any direction. Tears built up along my bottom eyelashes and the first broke free, splashing on the ground and turning the concrete the color of Dean's eyes.

"Do you have somewhere to go?"

I looked up, and Dean stood next to me again. I shook my head and another tear spilt.

"Come on then."

Dean and I both moved slowly. I jumped at every sound, expecting a gunshot or an Empath to burst out and attack us. Dean kept a steady pace but wobbled as he walked. He'd lost a fair bit of blood and must have felt woozy. I'd be woozy just from the pain with a hole in my arm like that. I offered my shoulder for support, and the second time, he accepted.

We only walked two blocks, to where a trailer park spread from the end of a cul-de-sac. Dean pulled out his keys and let us into a mid-sized trailer, permanently fixed in place like most others around it. The screen door rattled and inside a man lay sprawled across the couch. I stiffened and looked to Dean. He just shook his head, put a finger to his lips, and led me past a kitchenette piled in beer cans and a tiny bathroom to the room at the end. The man let out a gurgling snore as Dean closed the door behind us.

His room barely passed eight by eight feet in size, with a small bed, beanbag, and set of drawers taking up most of the space.

Dean scooped up an old towel from the floor and held it against his bleeding arm.

Boys. I frowned and snatched it off him. "Do you have any kind of first aid kit? Bandages or something? Alcohol? At least something *washed*? If you won't go to a doctor, we better clean that up properly ourselves."

Dean left the room. He returned with a box of band-aids, scissors, a clean cotton dishcloth and a bottle of vodka with just a finger or two left in the bottom.

He handed them to me and shrugged, then sat down on the side of the bed.

"Okay, we can work with this. Can you take your jacket and shirt off?"

Dean looked away, almost as though he was shy.

"I just mean, I might need to cut them off around your arm if you can't."

"No, I think I can manage."

Dean let out a slow hiss of air as he peeled the jacket away from the wound. I helped him pull the sleeves free of his wrists since he worked one-handed to undress. He tugged his t-shirt off over his head. It took him a while so I cut the dishcloth lengthways down the middle, and started working around in a zigzag line to turn one half into a long strip. I dropped the makeshift bandage on the bed and soaked the other half of the cloth in vodka.

Clenching my teeth against nausea, I bent forward to inspect his arm. A mixture of running, dried and coagulated blood created a gory mess. I dabbed around where it sat on his upper bicep until I could see the bullet hole clearly. I leaned so close to Dean I felt his body heat radiating off him and his breath against my face. The smell of blood mixed with the smoky-musk scent I noticed on him before.

With the blood cleared, I saw a clean hole passing straight through the edge of his muscle. Just half an inch and the bullet would have missed him completely. A couple of inches the other way and I didn't want to think about it. I just finished cleaning it off and it started bleeding again.

Dean spoke, his voice low. "You okay? You're turning all kinds of green."

I nodded but didn't open my mouth to reply, worried I might throw up.

I stood back up, away from the blood, and took a deep breath. I held up the bloody wash cloth. "You have another clean one?"

Dean told me where to look in the kitchen, and I cut the second in half as well to make some padding for the entry and exit spots. Then I started wrapping.

I felt Dean's eyes on me. I tried to focus on the bandaging.

"How about your cheek?" His breath as he spoke tickled the fine hairs on my neck.

"What about my cheek?"

Dean lifted his uninjured arm to the left side of my face, but didn't touch me. I placed a hand there myself and felt a sting. The first shot Jake fired. I remembered a pain on my cheek at the time, but then I saw the dead woman, and people started screaming and Jake kept pointing his gun… I'd completely forgotten about it. I noticed my hands shaking as I looped the bandage around Dean's arm.

"Is it bad? How's it look?"

"A thin line, just a graze I guess. Doesn't look like it bled much. You were lucky."

My first aid results looked pretty dismal when I'd done. I stuck the bandage closed with half a dozen adhesive band-aids. At least it didn't seem to be bleeding through yet.

I sighed and tried to wipe blood from my hands with the already soiled cloth. "Yeah, well, we both must be lucky since we're not dead. You should have just run. You wouldn't have been shot at all. Why didn't you run?"

Another shrug. No emotion I could read in his face or body language. He stood up and pulled a clean t-shirt from the drawers near the bed. He faced the other way as he put his shirt on in slow, careful movements. Muscles on his back shifted under the skin and I noticed how nice his body was. With the baggy clothes he wore I'd had no idea. I blushed, a mixture of embarrassment for staring and anger at my thoughts. How I'd stared so lustfully at the Empaths' attractive bodies. Them and their work-out routines, creating those pretty shells.

"You work out?" I asked, sounding cattier than I meant to.

Dean finally had the shirt over his shoulders and let it drop loose to cover his chest. He turned back toward me, eyebrow raised. "I *work*. I do some cash in hand jobs for a construction company. Manual labor stuff."

My thoughts became ragged. I was so angry at myself it overflowed onto Dean. I had no one to blame for my part but myself, but if Dean hadn't been at the bank, maybe guns would never have come out.

It would have been in and out. Easy pickings like Emma said. No one would have gotten shot. No one would have died.

“Why were you even at the bank? Were you following me?” I snapped.

Even without being able to read his emotions, I could tell from Dean’s frown just how dumb I’d been. The bank wasn’t far from the mall and park, but we drove, and went around in circles for ages while I got my wig right. Dean could have walked to the bank in that time, but couldn’t have followed us in Donnie’s jeep.

“The world doesn’t revolve around you,” he said. “I don’t know where you’re from, but this is my town, that was my bank. I was in to cash my dad’s welfare check. I try and do it myself if I can so it doesn’t all go on… my dad.”

The shake in my hands had spread up my back, up my throat and my head shook as I tried to apologize, for everything.

Dean talked over me. “Who were those guys? What was the trigger-happy fashion model talking about, about blockers and powers? Why was he set on shooting me? And don’t tell me it’s complicated.”

“They’re Empaths, like superheroes, but they weren’t superheroes. I just thought they were superheroes and that I was like them and I went with them but they weren't, they were the bad guys, and you're something else as well that does stuff to our super powers..." I kept babbling. I shook and tears streamed down my face, stinging the graze on my cheek.

Dean put his hands on my shoulders and I rattled under his touch. "Okay, crazy lady, you're really freaking out."

He steered me to the unmade bed and sat me down. I scooted across to sit with my back against the wall and pulled the covers up around me, trying to fight the chill racing through me.

"Put the TV on and just try and relax a bit. You're in shock. I'll go make you something hot."

I squinted at the small, blocky television sitting on the cluttered top of the drawers. "Where's the remote?"

"Doesn't have one."

"Really? Retro much. You can't even give this kind of box away anymore. I know. My mom's tried." I tried to smile a bit and lighten the mood, but my teeth chattered and I must have looked a little insane. I imagined how my hair must look after its release from under the wig and the mental image rounded out nicely.

"It's a whole two feet away. I'm sure you can manage."

Dean had made me a hot chocolate by the time I worked out how to get the television on and set the volume low, worried I'd wake his dad.

Dean went to take a hot shower, to shake off his own shock. I told him to keep his bandages dry if he could, but didn't know if that would help.

I settled into the blankets with the mug of hot goodness balanced on my knees and my shaking became less intense. I still felt teary, confused, and sick to my stomach. The news report on the TV didn't help.

The bank robbery was the top story. They showed some security camera footage, but too distant and grainy to make out any details. I had been right, though. The old woman Jake shot was dead. Was that my fault? If I hadn't stepped in front of Jake and he hadn't swung the gun away… no, then Dean would be dead. If Dean wasn't there, they might never have brought out the guns. But if I hadn't drawn attention to him they might not have spotted him in the crowd. If I'd refused to go at all, the whole thing might not have escalated. Or Dean would have been dead. I was like a hamster on a wheel, going round and round. *I could go crazy thinking like this.*

I thought the news report was over, but it continued. Another scene I recognized, the warehouse fire. Warehouse fire and theft, apparently.

While the one building burned, valuable goods had been taken from others nearby. There was evidence of arson. The news reporter said police felt confident linking this event with the bank robbery and other crimes in the area over the last month. The pattern also matched crimes from a number of cities previously. They used the term 'terrorist cell' and I pulled the blankets up closer around my face.

I hadn't even questioned Donnie and Jamie loading the car at the fire, or the extra luggage when we flew back from my home town. They were looters, but worse, even setting up disasters to take advantage of the emotions, making bad stuff happen on purpose. Not once had I seen them do anything heroic. I just assumed they did and they let me believe. Even Jake. I doubted whether he would have even saved me if I wasn't one of *them*. He said he saw some of the fight before he helped. How long did he wait and watch until he decided to help, to make sure I was one of them, just because he wanted another 'path on his team?

I heard the shower still running through the thin wall between Dean's room and the bathroom. Dean was shot. *I* was shot. Someone died. It was a mess and it didn't even faze Jake. Just what else had he done in the past?

I had to stop them. The only way Dean and any other victims of these villains could be safe was to shut the team down. Permanently. Block off their powers for good.

Jake said Dean could do that. How? I had no idea. Dean probably wouldn't know either. He might not even want to help. I finished the hot chocolate and put the mug on the drawers next to the TV. My eyelids felt leaden and sound of the running water calmed me.

But Dean could learn how to shut down Empaths. He could practice on me. I would give up my powers. I'd give up the whole super hero fantasy if it meant everyone would be safe again.

I stared at the screen of my phone. I'd been staring for half an hour since I woke up, according to the clock. I'd tapped in my home number but couldn't hit Call.

Dean slept on the beanbag. I'd fallen asleep in his bed before he got out of the shower. He curled on one side, holding the bandage on his arm with the other hand. It didn't look comfortable. I noticed no coldness from him while he slept, but couldn't read any emotions from him either. That could just be because he was asleep. What did I know? It wasn't like I'd had training with this stuff.

I sighed and looked at my phone again. I should call my parents, but at this point what could I say? *Sorry for leaving, I'll be back as soon as I take down a bunch of super-powered criminals.* Yeah, that wouldn't freak them out at all.

The beans in the beanbag rustled and hissed like a snake. Dean shifted and opened his eyes. I gave him a shy smile in return. He probably felt more awkward with me here in his bed than I felt. I could only make guesses though, as the coldness crept into me again.

I put the phone down on the top of the drawers.

"Morning. You calling someone?" he asked.

"I was going to call my parents." I took a deep breath. Time to sell Dean on my plan. "But I want to finish all of this first."

I started again, trying to explain the Empath powers, who Jake and the team were, and what Jake said about Dean being a blocker.

Dean still looked skeptical.

"I know you think I was babbling like a madman last night, but it's real, the powers, the whole thing."

"Then show me."

"I *can't.* You're a blocker remember? When you're around, you stop my powers from working. At least unless you're surprised by something and let go a bit."

"I'm not doing anything on purpose."

"I know. But I need you to believe me. I need your help. Let's go outside and I'll see what sort of range the blocking has. Maybe I can demonstrate from a distance. I'll still need some strong emotion to tap, though. Anger emotions are easiest."

"Sure, okay. But you probably shouldn't go out looking like that."

Dean dropped his gaze to my chest and I blushed. Then I looked down too and saw the bloodstains across the front of my shirt. Dean dug out what he assured me was his smallest t-shirt and I went into the bathroom to change and clean up.

I tried to tuck the shirt in, tie it to the side, do anything to make it not look like I wore a tent. Nothing worked, so I just wore it untucked.

Dean paused and looked me over before we left the trailer. "Looks good on you."

He said it in the same matter-of-fact way he'd complimented my smile before. I just shook my head and tried to cool my face. I never understood why guys liked girls wearing their shirts. Wearing a guy's t-shirt felt like the most unflattering fashion ever.

It wasn't too early, but no one else seemed to be out and about in the trailer park. Finding some anger to tap proved easy. Just a few trailers down the sounds of a domestic came clearly though thin walls. I stood outside, and Dean backed away until I felt the cold leave me and gave him a thumbs up.

I let the heat of emotion radiate into me and my muscles burned with strength. A 'Caution Children' sign across the laneway became my target for a demonstration.

I checked Dean was still watching, grabbed the pole with both hands and put my foot against the middle. I pulled with my hands and pushed with my foot, and the solid metal pole bent in half.

It felt good to be so effective with my powers and I couldn't resist a smile when I saw Dean's jaw drop in the distance. I probably looked the same when Jake demonstrated his powers by smashing that bench. Ugh. Way to break a mood. I didn't even care then how much work someone must have put into the careful mosaic artwork on the bench Jake destroyed without a second thought. Neither did Jake. He just demolished it to make a point. *I should have known then what I was getting into.* But I'd been blinded by surface things, not to mention dazzled by an Empath much better at this stuff than I was.

I strained to straighten the pole, which proved harder than bending it in the first place.

A red flash in the corner of my eye made me look down the long laneway through the trailer park toward the road that passed the other end. Jake's Maserati cruised by at a speed designed for scoping.

I dashed back to Dean as fast as I could until my powers waned in his presence again. I still had just enough momentum left when I reached him to drag him out of the middle of the lane and into the cover of the nearest trailer.

"Okay, I believe you!"

"No, it's them, the car down there."

The Maserati continued on, and we snuck back to the sanctuary of Dean's room.

The minor effort of our excursion left Dean looking paler than normal. Some blood showed through his bandage, and I worried it wasn't healing right.

He took a seat on his bed and I paced while I presented my plan to block Jake and his team's powers for good. As I thought, Dean had no idea how to even begin.

"That's why I want you to practice on me. You can learn how to do it by locking away my powers."

He didn't respond. He just stared with the usual blank expression.

"Look, I know it's a lot to ask making you learn how to do this and take on those guys, but you saw how dead set Jake was to get rid of you. It's the only thing I can think of to keep you and others safe. Without, you know, turning to assassination or something. We can't even call the cops on them, not while they still have their powers."

Dean nodded. "I understand. I can try, but it still feels kind of crazy. I don't even know where to start."

"Me neither. We just experiment I guess." I slumped down onto the beanbag. "I only really found out about my own powers last week. I know less about yours. When I use mine, it feels like sun warming my skin, spreading heat through me. When you're around I just feel cold."

Dean made a face. Normally I would know exactly what that meant, but without my powers as far as I knew the emotion could be anything from anger to just-passed-gas.

"I just mean, if energy is warm, it's like a cold lack of energy. Can you, I don't know, try and project more coldness?"

It felt stupid even as the words came out of my mouth, but Dean tried anyway. I could see him concentrating, but nothing changed. We gave up and had toast for lunch.

Dean's dad wasn't around and we sat in the living room. It smelled of stale alcohol.

"Why are we even like this? How do these powers work? If I understand them more we might get further," Dean said with his mouth full.

"Well, for Empaths, we just sort of absorb excess emotion from people and it makes us stronger."

"So you're kind of like vampires, feeding on other people's life force."

"That's silly."

"Fine, leeches then, or parasites. I mean, excess? You really think people don't need every bit of the emotions they are feeling? That anything you can tap into is just spare?"

"I…" I hadn't thought of it like that. "I just thought the powers were part of being a hero."

Dean had inhaled his toast the way boys do and pushed crumbs around the empty plate with his finger. "Pretty people, hot cars, wads of spending money… Was that your idea of being a hero, too?"

"Just the perks?" I fake smiled, toothy and pleading. I was being lectured, but I deserved it. Dean had a way of seeing things I'd been blind to. I needed to hear what he thought. "What is your idea of a hero?"

"Someone who doesn't think about themselves, who puts others first always, even before their own life. Someone like…"

Dean stood up without warning and dumped his empty plate into the sink. He paused there for a moment then came back to sit next to me on the couch. I chewed my toast slowly and stared at the floor.

"I wish I knew how you were feeling." Why did I say that out loud? I blushed and rambled on. "I just mean, you block all your feelings away for whatever reason, so much it extends out and blocks Empath powers too. If I knew more about how, or why, it might help."

Dean made eye contact for a moment before returning his focus to the stained carpet.

"If you could work out how to let emotions out a little, it might be easier to also pull them in more, create a more powerful block than your normal one. Something that could lock down an Empath permanently, like Jake said blockers can do. Do you think you could try letting some emotion through?"

Dean shook his head. "I don't think I can just... do that."

My suggestions weren't working and Dean seemed less and less interested in trying them. But he had let emotions through in the past, or at least had been surprised out of holding them back so much they blocked my powers. In the alley, and when he was shot, he was too shocked to keep a tight rein on his feelings. I hadn't actually read his emotions those times, but I hadn't exactly tried. Other things on my mind and all. If I could just surprise him again now, I could see what happened.

I don't know why I thought the first idea that popped into my head seemed legit, but I acted on the impulse before common sense or embarrassment could stop me. I leaned over to Dean next to me on the lounge and pressed my lips against his. They were soft and cool and spread slightly under mine. My eyes fluttered closed and a shiver crept over my scalp. I felt the coldness leave me and opened my eyes, surprised my impulsive action worked. Dean's gray eyes looked into mine, inches away, just as surprised.

I focused on reading any emotions I could in them, drawing them into me. What I felt was heavy with depression, hiding something smaller, tentative and warm. Something guarded even closer. I moved my lips back away from Dean's. His breath was fast and hot on my face.

The depression I tapped overwhelmed me, like a heavy weight around my chest dragging me into black water. I backed away to the other end of the couch, shaking my head like I'd just been boxed in the ears. "Too much… bad feelings…"

Dean felt confused, hurt, and then the icy chill spread through me again and I couldn't read him anymore.

"You did that just to get my guard down?"

"And it worked, yay? I'm sorry, it was the first plan that came to me. Your emotions were just a bit much for me. But I'm sorry, anyway. I shouldn't have done that, or I should have asked first. No wait, that wouldn't have worked, duh-doy."

Dean had closed off completely. He didn't look sad, or upset. He didn't even look angry. But now I knew inside he kept hidden a deep well of grief. Pressed down, out of sight. I could tell his life wasn't easy. Everything around us screamed poverty. His dad didn't seem to work, and was probably an alcoholic, but Dean came across as smart, and able, and so… kind.

I tried to smooth things over with Dean. He didn't talk much for the rest of the day, but remained cooperative, nodding and trying a few more suggestions. We tried some visualizing techniques but honestly they just felt wanky. It was still early when Dean started looking gray and tired, and I could tell his arm troubled him. We ended the day frustrated and without any headway on locking down my powers.

I insisted Dean kept his own bed and I curled up on the beanbag. He fell asleep before me, and for a while, before I found my own rest, I stared at him, remembering the sensation of the deep, black despair he kept inside.

Thursday morning I woke up to Dean trying to tiptoe around me.

"What time is it?" I asked, squinting at the window. The mostly bent blinds were still drawn but barely any light came in.

"Six thirty. I need to get to work." Dean put on a dark blue hoody with holes at the elbows. "I'll be back about three."

I bolted upright in the beanbag. It shifted under me and I almost fell on my side.

"No, you can't. If you're out working all day Jake might find you."

"I have to work, Livvy. I didn't even get to cash Dad's welfare check this week and I'm out of money."

Not only had I been taking up all his time, eating his food, and getting him in trouble in the first place, it was my fault he couldn't get to work or a bank. He couldn't work now anyway, not manual labor.

"No, I won't take any arguments. You can't go, not with your arm like that. I bet it's hurting."

Dean sat down again with a slight wince.

"Yeah, I thought as much. Can I have a look at your arm? We should put a clean dressing on it. Or at least that's what people seem to do in movies. Then you can walk me into town and I'll see about some cash."

"And that will be safer than me going to work?"

I couldn't really blame him for thinking the worst. "I'm not going to rob a bank if that's what you're thinking. And at least if I'm with you, I could knock you out or something and use my powers to get us out of there if things go wrong. If you show up at your job with a bullet hole through your arm, people are going to talk and Jake will find out who you are and where to find you."

"Well, you have worked out one way to shock me out of my blocking ability," Dean mumbled.

I blushed and went to get more makeshift first aid supplies. Once I got some cash in town I'd get some real bandages and dressings.

I unwrapped and cleaned Dean's arm. It hadn't gotten any better, and the skin around it looked red and inflamed. I bandaged the wound with the last clean washcloth available in the trailer and Dean walked me into town. *I should probably buy him some more washcloths as well.*

It proved hard trying to walk casually while still keeping an eye out in all directions for Jake or the rest of his team. We made it to the main street without any sign of them. The bank was closed up, police tape webbed across the front flapping in the slight breeze. I went into the pawn shop I saw last time I was here and sold my heart pendant necklace. I got less than half what I knew my parents had paid, but it was something, enough to get by a couple more days.

I asked Dean about somewhere to get lunch, and he took me around the corner to a tucked away diner with a drug store conveniently next door. I bought a cheap first aid kit which had alcohol swabs, bandages and dressings then went into the diner, insisting on buying lunch for us both.

The diner had a mix of cracking plastic table sets and a line of tall booths along the wall. It was still early for lunch so the place was practically empty and we took a booth in the far back corner.

I bullied Dean into ordering something substantial, and after I'd paid I slid the remainder of the cash across the table.

"What's that?" He was already shaking his head.

"It's for you."

"I can't take that."

"Sure you can. It's your pay. I'm paying you to work for me, to keep trying to do this blocking thing. If you can't get to your job because of me, then I'm your job."

We locked gazes, both unwilling to budge with the money sitting on the table.

The waitress brought our food over and raised an eyebrow at our strange stand-off. She put a massive hamburger down in front of Dean, and milkshakes that came in tall retro glasses. My fish and fries were in an actual basket, already spotted with grease from previous meals.

I smiled at the waitress then pouted. "I'm trying to pay him back and he won't take it."

She wiped her hands on her apron and flicked her curly hair. "Just take the cash, kid, before I consider it a tip."

Dean pocketed the money begrudgingly and the waitress left us to our food.

"You didn't have to sell your pendant. Didn't it mean something to you?"

"Other things mean more."

I picked through the fries and battered fish bits. They were good but I didn't have a big appetite. Dean seemed to barely be putting up with my presence.

I wasn't surprised considering the trouble I'd brought him, not to mention crashing his house and sleeping in his room. Each day he seemed more and more irritated sharing close quarters with me. Or maybe it was my crazy plan and nagging to get this to work. But it had to work. At every moment I worried Jake would find Dean, or go to my parents to find me. He had to be stopped before he hurt anyone else.

Back in the trailer after lunch we sat in the living room and tried again to practice his blocking abilities. We attempted turning them off and on, making them stronger or weaker, but nothing worked.

Dean's wound bled through again so I rewrapped it with real dressings and the result looked a lot better. I hoped that meant it would also heal better. I didn't like the way it was looking one bit.

Dean was just putting his shirt back on when his dad stumbled in the front door.

"Just finishing up with your little whore?" His words sounded slurred.

I winced. Great, an angry drunk. *I like him better when he's passed out and snoring.*

"Dad, don't." Dean stood up as a buffer between the two of us.

His dad's gray hair was greasy and while his eyes were the same shade as Dean's, they bulged, bloodshot, and gave him the look of a crazy man. They fixed on me over Dean's shoulder.

"I know you sniffing around last few days. I see it's going on. Don't think you can go shacking up here. No money to be sniffing for anyway, and you can't be having more of my drink."

I opened my mouth but just shook my head. I looked to Dean for a cue on what I should do, worried how embarrassed he might be. I got nothing. I might as well have been a figment of his dad's drunken imagination.

Dean put a hand on his dad's shoulder, leading him to the room at the opposite end to Dean's. "Why don't you go lie down for a while?"

His dad swatted the gesture away. "You two stole my vodka! Don't make excuses. I know what's what and what's gone. You get rid of that whore, Dean. Get her out before she goes leaves anyway! Just like your mom."

He turned the other way and left out the front door again, cursing and stumbling.

I sat speechless on the couch.

"Sorry." Dean stared at the closed front door and didn't look like he would turn around any time soon.

"Is that it? Is that why your dad's like that, because your mom left?" I blurted. I clenched my shaking fists. Dean hadn't stood up for me, just let his dad call me a whore, rant like that to my face.

Dean remained still. "She didn't leave. She died."

"Oh, crap. No, I mean, I'm-" Sorry didn't cut it. I was such an idiot.

"He wasn't always like that. He just couldn't handle the way she left." Dean leant on the back of the door and still didn't face me. I wanted to poke, to pry, to encourage him to keep talking, but decided keeping my mouth shut was the best option right now, in case another foot could fit in.

The silence extended and I thought he might not have anything else to say. He stayed leaning on the door. I stayed watching anxiously from the couch. Finally he spoke.

"My mom got sick. Like, never-getting-better sick. We weren't badly off and Dad gave everything, every saving, every dollar he'd earned on any kind of treatment he could find. Dad refused to let her go, refused to give in or stop doing whatever it took. The medical costs bankrupted us. We lost our house just to keep Mom in hospital in palliative care. She didn't want to be there. She faded, slowly, painfully, and steadily. She was ready to go and knew what the illness was doing to us."

Dean didn't move. His words were slow and held just the smallest edge of pain. I, on the other hand, mopped tears up with the neckline of Dean's t-shirt I was wearing. I kept quiet, didn't sob, but the tears just ran. The sadness I'd felt in Dean when I kissed him all came back to me. How long had his mother's illness gone on? What had their family been like before? What had Dean been like before? I'd never seen him really smile. I bet he was gorgeous if he really smiled. It would reach those gray eyes and they would sparkle in a way they never did now. The neck of my shirt was sodden.

Dean's next words came a moment after the others. His voice broke so slightly I wondered if it was my own imagination.

"Mom took her own life."

I'm sorry. They were such useless words, so flimsy. What everyone says when they don't know what to say.

I thought back to my parents and the strength of their love. If what happened to Dean's family happened to ours, under those circumstances, would they break? If I lost one of them, and then lost the other in a different way, I doubted I'd manage half as well Dean. I'd up and left them behind for this adventure gone wrong, but only because they were so permanent. Like no matter what I did, I could always go back to home, to comfort, and there they would be. Even when distant my parents were a safe place in my heart. The idea of losing that seared my insides.

I would lock all my emotions away too. Stop myself ever having to risk loving and losing anyone again.

Dean shifted and I wiped frantically at my face to dry it before he turned around.

"Thank you, for sharing that with me," I stuttered, hoping my words weren't completely useless. "Your mother was strong. I understand now what it means to be a hero."

He faced me and I shivered.

I grew colder inside than his presence had ever made me. Anything Dean had opened up, he'd now closed again tighter than ever before.

He sat back next to me on the lounge and asked about what we were going to try next.

I casually caught another tear with the flick of a finger and suggested we take a break and spend the rest of the day watching TV.

We sat close, our shoulders just touching enough to share warmth between us, but inside the sensation of cold only grew.

That night, I wriggled myself into a semi-comfortable position on the beanbag again before Dean could say anything about sleeping arrangements. He came back in from his shower and stood still in the middle of the room for a moment before getting into his bed.

"I'm sorry," he said. "For being angry that night we first met. For not saying thank you for what you did."

I didn't know what to say. I had obsessed over it at the time, but when everything went crazy I'd forgotten about it again until he brought it up. It just didn't seem to mean so much anymore. "That was you angry? I was the one yelling like a lunatic."

"I was angry, and I'm sorry."

"It's okay, really."

Dean paused, his jaw clenching briefly. "It's just, I saw this mousy girl-"

"Hey!"

"-willing to take on two big guys, willing to risk herself to save a stranger. To do something like that, you have to be someone really special. It made me so angry, the thought that someone so special could have been hurt, for someone like me."

Neither of us said anything else.

I hadn't done it for him. I'd done it for myself, to feel like a hero, to be praised. I had no idea what it meant to be a hero, not then.

The next morning, I woke up and saw Dean sitting on the side of his bed, watching me. Something inside felt different, a turmoil of hot and cold, and then it came.

Ice grew in me, crystallizing and encasing every sensation of Empath power I knew. And then I felt nothing at all. Not the warmth of the power, not the cold of Dean's blocking. Nothing.

I ran through the trailer park, trying to connect to any emotion outside of my own but nothing came.

It was done. I was normal.

At night, the overgrown park across from the mall felt like a scene from Grimm's fairy tales. The wooden play fortress loomed in shadows and the slight breeze made tree branches creak against each other. Only one street light at either end of the park provided lighting, and both flickered. It was cold and I pulled the fleecy jacket Dean had given me around me tight. It smelled of him and my heart beat a little faster.

I hoped the cold would give us an advantage, so Jake and his posse wouldn't sense what was happening until too late.

I'd called Jake earlier that day. He wasn't happy to hear from me, and I begged, I begged shamelessly to be given another chance to be part of their team again.

I wondered what time it was, whether the team was late. I felt like I'd been here hours. But Dean and I did get here much earlier than we needed, to give Dean a chance to get hidden before the agreed meeting time.

The hiding spot looked uncomfortable, particularly with his arm still hurting him so much. He suggested the park while I tried to think of somewhere with a place Dean could hide, public but without other people around. Somewhere that wouldn't seem more suspicious to the team than I thought this already must.

Dean knew the park well, with its special hiding place that only local kids knew.

A car pulled up beside the park. Not one of the team's usual favorites, but it was them. My blond prince charming who had turned from beauty to beast strolled up followed by his pack. They seemed confident and I sighed inwardly. It meant we cleared the first part of the plan I'd worried about. Dean was able to hold in his blocking power. If he hadn't been able, the team would have sensed him as soon as they arrived. I'd only realized it could be an issue after he'd already locked me down, so we had no way to test he could do it. But Dean seemed confident. He said he'd worked something out. He had something inside now he could use to control his abilities. Now I just had to hope he could keep holding in his general block and still individually shut each of the team down for good.

Jake wore a dark leather jacket over a stark white designer shirt. He stared at me with disdain. I marveled at the face I once thought so dreamy that now spoke of nightmares.

"So, hi." Lame. I had to get my brain working, keep them engaged, talking, so Dean had time to do his part. But seeing Jake and the team flicked the off switch in my head. I shivered and it had nothing to do with the cold.

"Living rough, honey?" Emma smirked at my outfit. She, of course, looked ready to hit a catwalk, mini dress, stiletto heels and all.

"Yeah, things have sucked." That was a direction I could take, playing to their egos. "But it was good to see what it's like without you. And it was basically a whole lot of sucking."

Jamie, looking like a mini version of Jake, chuckled. "That's what she said."

Jake held up a hand, silencing his brother, and glared at me some more. "So you think you can manage it now, doing what we do? You want it bad enough? Not going to flip out like a freak again and mess up our plans? You got us into all kinds of trouble with your stunt."

"I'm sorry." The words tasted disgusting in my mouth, but I worked to keep my emotions stable. "I know I screwed things up."

Donnie looked more and more uncomfortable as we spoke. He tried to get Jake's attention a couple of times but Jake kept shushing him, too busy enjoying a good gloat at my expense. *Come on, Dean.*

"And why should we even want to bring you back in?" Jake strode around me in a circle. He must be able to tell how uncomfortable this whole situation made me. I hoped he thought it was just nerves in his oh-so-glorious presence, the bastard.

He came to a stop behind my back. He groaned softly. "What is that? I feel..."

Donnie looked drained. "I've been trying to tell you, something's happening. I think the blocker is here."

Jake grabbed me and turned me to face him, shaking me. "Is he here? Did you bring him here?"

Last ditch effort. "It's probably just the cold you're feeling."

Donnie looked around frantically. "I think he's locked me down. I've lost it all."

Jake shoved me and yelled at the others. "Find him! He's got to be close by."

Jamie moved in a flash. I guess Dean hadn't gotten to him yet. He sprinted around the park, checking the perimeter, behind trees and fences, in high grass.

Donnie moved slower. He went to the play equipment and wooden fort. I tensed, and tried not to watch and make it obvious where Dean hid. Climbing through it, Donnie's adult footsteps clunked heavily on the timber. I hoped for a plank to snap under his weight but no such luck. Still, they weren't finding Dean.

Emma watched Donnie's slow, normal movements for a moment with her mouth agape. "I can't. I can't lose my powers. I can't go back."

She fled, just a blur till she reached their car, and took off in it on her own. Quite a feat in the shoes she wore.

Jake pulled a gun from the behind his back. He pointed it at me, and his hand shook. "I'm not losing this power, Livvy. You're dying first."

I knew Jake wouldn't be shy about turning to guns. My plan was to keep Dean safe until Jake and his crew were all locked down, then they could be the cops' problem. Dean didn't like it, with him hiding and me in the firing line, so I came up with a plan comforting Dean's concerns for me, but to be honest, I wasn't so sold on it. Right now I had few other options. Without my powers I was already at a disadvantage, and I didn't have firearms as a fallback.

"You can't shoot me. If I don't get back safe by midnight, you're done. I've given that phone you gave me to someone, and if I don't see them again, they will turn it in to the cops, along with all your numbers, that lovely happy snap of us and notes on all of you and your activities."

Jake's face became a feral mix of snarl and smile. "You think I care about that? I've still got plenty of cash to get away clear and can change my face if I have to. But I won't have to. I will still have my powers, and with my powers *I* am the law. You hear that out there, Blocker?" Jake called out into the park where Donnie and Jamie still hadn't found Dean. He kept the gun held in front of my face. "If you shut me down, this girl is dead. Crawl out of wherever you're hiding and we can all just sort this out."

A low wall in the base of the wooden fortress shifted, just within the join of two sections of the construction; a gap that had been badly patched up when the original builder's plans didn't line up quite right creating the perfect hiding place.

"Dean, don't!"

The wall hinged open, revealing a standing room only space and Dean stepped out and walked toward us, holding his hands up in a gesture of surrender.

Jake whipped his gun away from me and fired.

No hesitation, no time to stop him, no time to talk him out of it, no time for anything.

He shot Dean, just like that.

I ran to Dean, but it felt like a dream where everything was too slow.

A look of shock hung on Dean's face and he stopped still. He stared at his chest like he couldn't believe the way the blood pooled and spread across the fabric of his shirt. Like he'd spilled ketchup on himself, and might just laugh with embarrassment and brush it off. Then his legs buckled.

I ran. I was too slow.

I skidded under Dean just before his head hit the ground, catching it in my lap. But I had been too slow to have stopped the bullet, pushed him out of the way, saved him.

Dean's skin was more blue than pale. He kept his teeth clenched, panting between them.

"Help!" I screamed into the night uselessly. If the gunshot hadn't brought anyone, my scream wouldn't either.

"Liv?" Dean grasped for one of my hands. "Listen. I'm sorry."

His chest bled so much.

I let out a wheezing cry.

"For pushing you away. Being scared of you. Of feeling for you."

Jake yelled at me. "Stand back up, Livvy. I want you facing me."

I didn't want to hear him. I only wanted to hear Dean, to keep hearing him talk so I knew he was still okay. I cradled Dean's head and he held me trapped in the gaze of his gray eyes.

"Didn't want to feel like that. That risk of losing someone I needed again. The feeling was, is, too intense. Shutting it down gave me what I needed to control these powers. But I don't want to anymore, don't want to shut it down. Not if I'm dying. I want you to know."

"You're not going to die. Good guys don't die," I sobbed.

"Livvy," Dean breathed.

My chest burned. The fierceness of what I felt for Dean scorched through me, the pain and pure need. And not just mine. It came from Dean as well, warming me throughout like a nearby fire.

Arms, hard like steel, yanked me away from Dean and I screamed like I'd been torn apart. Jamie pinned me up against him, pulling me away. I kicked and wrenched my body around but his grip was charged by emotion. Emotion he stole from me. My pain.

Jamie dragged me back toward Jake, but he felt weaker and weaker.

No. I was stronger.

Any ice inside had melted away and power unfurled within me, wild and mighty. Dean had unlocked my powers again, by sharing this warmth. I could fight back, get help for Dean, save him. There was still time. *Please, please let there be enough time.*

I tore one arm free of Jamie's grip and turned so I could see Dean on the ground again.

I had to let him know everything was going to be okay.

His eyes were closed, and body gave a startling shudder then went still.

I let out a sound between a scream and a roar.

I'd fallen in love with him. Had he been trying to tell me he felt the same? And he was dying, or already dead.

I ripped into Jamie, who still tried to keep hold of me. Donnie came to help him, unpowered, but still strong and half my size again. I sparred back, ducking their blows and kicking, scratching, jabbing between them with more strength than they could ever know. I drew the power from myself, from the fury of my own emotions, not stealing the scraps from others.

Jake kept his gun aimed our way, but didn't fire at the risk of hitting one of his own. I was surprised he had even that much moral fiber. He stashed the gun and came to join in by hand.

Love gave me the strength to keep all three men at bay.

But the pain…

Dean taught me what it meant to be a hero, a real hero. He taught me I didn't need some fake fairytale hero to dream of, that I could be the hero. But I couldn't save him, the one person I wanted to save the most.

Jake caught me with a blow to my jaw that slid me back along the ground. I didn't even feel it. I launched myself at the men again. I broke ribs, snapped knees, pulled arms from their sockets. I fought for my life and for Dean's, if it was still there.

I knew despair like I never had, like I couldn't begin to handle. A black, bottomless pool threatening to drown drew me in like quicksand. Dean still didn't move. He looked dead.

Darkness overwhelmed me, and the despair fed on everything I had inside, consuming any feelings of morality or mercy. And it remained ravenous.

I turned it on Jake, Jamie and Donnie and let it feed. I used the black energy to tear every power and every emotion from their bodies. They fell to the ground like human husks. Just pretty shells.

I stumbled a few steps towards Dean's body, completely burnt out.

Then I fell too.

Everything was too bright. Light, noise, beeping, and why was everyone screaming?

I stirred, and when I opened my eyes I found myself in a hospital bed, strung up with tubes running from my wrist and wires stuck to my chest.

A petite dark-skinned nurse leant over me to press the call button.

She smiled at me as I blinked myself awake. My head pounded and I winced.

"There you are. Careful now, you've been out for a while. We'll get a doctor in to look you over as soon as we can."

Her smile hit me like a solid wall of energy, the strength of her happiness making me nauseous. Who was ever that cheery? All around me emotions seeped through the walls from people celebrating, people grieving, people fighting enemies in their own bodies to stay alive. Every emotion invaded me, crawled into me like tiny spiders digging under my skin. I rolled over to the side of the bed.

The nurse must have seen me turn green because she was ready with a pan to catch my vomit.

A doctor came in, accompanied by a man in a suit who showed me his detective badge. I leaned back in the bed and took deep breaths, trying to slow the spinning inside. The doctor started checking me and my attached machines and said I didn't have to talk to the cop yet if I didn't want to.

I shook my head only slightly but it hummed with pain. "What happened? Is Dean…?"

The detective took a seat next to my bed and pulled out a note pad. "We were hoping you could tell us what happened. No one else has been able, and the scene we found, with one boy shot and you and three others injured and unconscious, well, I've never seen anything like it. We've identified the shooter from the bank robbery, and the two other men carrying guns as his associates. Now we're just trying to work out how you and the boy who was shot come into it."

My mind raced over all the evidence of my involvement with Jake's team. Photos, phone calls, texts, leaving home, my stuff at their place, the video from the bank. I had to tell the truth, as much as would be believed. I had to tell this detective I didn't realize who Jake and his companions were until it was too late. It was going to be a long story, and long investigation, and I couldn't handle it now. I could barely think.

I looked the cop in the eye and knew I could manipulate him, make him think and do what I wanted, the way Jake had done to me. He may not be physically attracted to me, but power rushed through me and emotions blazed from him I could use to smooth through all his defenses.

I turned my head away and asked if the detective could come back later. I'd tell him everything he wanted to know when I was better. *If I ever got better.*

He nodded and gave the side of my bed a sympathetic pat. "Of course. Whenever you're ready. Anything you can give me to help me understand what happened, I'd appreciate it. We've got enough evidence on the three men to tie them to a number of crimes in the area, but the confusing part is they either seem to be trying for an insanity plea or are actually mentally disabled. Catatonic, all three of them."

I could tell him what happened, now I realized what I'd done. I'd killed them. Or I might as well have. I ripped all their emotions right from their bodies, leaving them as vegetables.

I bent over the side of the bed again, my eyes watering and chest convulsing. The nurse held a pan out for me again and I retched, but nothing came up. My body rolled inside with pain and guilt and I wished I could vomit it all out, clear all these feelings from me.

I had taken lives.

Their powers I had somehow absorbed, stolen. That's why everything was amplified. I deserved this torment, the screaming of every emotion around me drilling into my skull. It could send me insane, and I almost hoped it did. I only had to know one thing first.

My voice was a harsh scratch, and I spoke to the floor, still bent over the side of the bed. "Did he die? Is Dean dead?"

My heart grew small and painfully tight waiting for the answer.

The nurse replied. "He's been in and out of consciousness since surgery. He almost-"

I was already moving, throwing back the sheets, tearing drips and wires off me.

The nurse tried to talk me down. The doctor stepped in front of me to urge me back to bed. I shoved him weakly, and he flew across and hit the wall with a smack, bringing a beeping machine down with him. Stronger than I realized, I clenched my teeth as my body ran riot with overloaded emotional power.

I bolted down corridors, not giving a thought to the state of my hospital robe. I followed my nose, or rather, my heart, and found myself at ICU. I stumbled into the room Dean lay in, grabbed his hand and dropped my head onto his shoulder.

I found quiet there.

Next to Dean, the pains and pleasures of others bellowing around me were muffled. I found myself weeping with relief.

"Hey." Dean's voice was dry and husky.

"You're alive. You're awake," I whispered into his shoulder.

"Yeah, you too."

I didn't feel any cold, just soothing warmth. He wasn't holding back. He wasn't keeping any of his emotions from me, but still calmed me with the abilities he'd learned.

The love I sensed from him made me weep more, but happily. I wished he could experience how I felt for him in return.

I lifted my head from his shoulder and kissed him.

The kiss was gentle, lingering, and I put everything into it that I couldn't give justice to in words. It tasted of salt tears and summer days, heating us both with glowing joy and desire.

He put a hand around my waist and pulled me onto the bed next to him. He let out a small grunt of pain when I pressed against him but kissed me harder.

I pulled my lips away just far enough to talk. "I'm sorry. You okay?"

"Worth it." He smiled like I'd never seen before and his gray eyes sparkled as they stared into mine.

I heard shuffling near the door but couldn't turn my eyes away from Dean's.

"Livvy?"

It was my mom. A jolt of worry from her was enough to pull me back from Dean to face her and Dad. They came in and hugged me. I tried not to break them when I squeezed them back.

The army of hospital staff I'd tackled through to reach Dean looked over their shoulders, demanding obedience and answers. My parents got rid of them with a few firm words and we were left in peace.

I still clung to Dean's hand and my parents explained the hospital called them when they identified me. They said they'd been so worried when I disappeared, but my 'friend' explained I'd be away for a while. It seemed to make sense at first, but as time passed they couldn't understand why they'd accepted his explanation. When they found out I was in the hospital it almost killed them.

They had questions for me too. Lots of them.

"I made mistakes and fell in with the wrong crowd. I'm sorry. Please don't ask me too many questions. You won't like the answers. If we can just leave it at that, I promise I won't make those mistakes again."

Maybe one day I would explain more. My parents still embodied concern. They shared a look between them and nodded slowly. I saw my mom look at Dean, and our tightly joined hands.

"And this boy, was he part of the wrong crowd?" Her tone wasn't accusing. It was soft, tentative with care.

"No. He's the one who saved me. And I saved him."

Emotionally Scarred

~ Emma's Story ~

I wish I could use magic to stop people staring at me, or enchant myself to be beautiful, but the magic powers I have are different. I'm not really a witch, no matter what the other kids call me. I'm not a superhero either, even if I do have special powers. Heroes aren't ugly.

The lime-green shade of my new school's corridors set my teeth on edge. Everyone watched me, and why wouldn't they? I was the new girl with a target right on her face. My sneakers squeaked as I walked and I felt so completely conspicuous. Cruel laminate flooring. My own body betrayed me as well. I was taller than most girls, which just made me easier to spot. I wanted to love my bright red hair but I hated that it attracted attention to my face.

The other students stared openly at me and gossiped as they pretended to poke through their lockers. A tide of emotion followed their stares, the usual mix of sympathy and disgust that I was used to. That was my superpower — to sense how people were feeling, so strongly that I felt their emotions burrowing into my pores. I hated it. I hugged my new textbooks close to my chest and tried to ignore it.

Chin up, Emma. Don't let them get to you. You're beautiful on the inside. You're special and important, no matter how you look.

I tried to believe that my outer appearance didn't matter and that *real* friends would like the *real* me despite how I looked. But I was smart, smarter than most kids my age, and it made them think I was even weirder. My intelligence made me as much of a target as my face. I tried to act like everyone else, dress right, talk right, do all the right things. I had gone from being a child prodigy down to a C average. I stuffed tests on purpose, half-hearted my assignments, and worked harder on giggling mindlessly, and pretending I actually like music where dudes sing about their sexy bitches. Anything to just fit in.

It didn't work.

This year was supposed to be better. Operation: New Me. I finally convinced my parents to let me change schools. Well… by convinced, I mean I was expelled from my last school when I got into a fight with this girl who kept calling me names. I had a weird adrenaline rush and broke her arm. Oops.

A little extra begging on top and my parents finally let me have the mole, the bane of my existence, removed. The mole that had made me the brunt of bullying my whole life. This was no cute beauty mark, oh no, but a brown blob of ugly flesh that covered half my chin. That's why I was called a witch at my last school. Marked by the devil, dribbling sewage, fecal face; I heard it all from the other kids.

My life was a living hell. If they also knew I could read their emotions like some kind of freak…

But all that changed. I was going off to a new school, and in between, I'd have the mole removed. Then it was meant to be like in the books, where a group of great friends would adopt me and the hottest guy in the school would fall for me. I wouldn't be teased. I would be happy.

The whole plan plunged into epic fail. My plebian parents didn't realize I needed a proper cosmetic surgeon for the work, to actually make my face look like the mole was never there. Sure the doctor removed the mole, but in its place he left a jumbo pink scar like a deformed fetus.

Determined to be positive anyway, I came to this new school with a plan. I dressed up, smiled, and waited for people to ask, wow, where did you get that scar? And I would tell them crazy cool tales of my heroism, saving a baby girl from a pit bull attack, only to have a chunk of flesh bitten off my face. I'd say it was nothing, I did what I had to do to save a child. Beloved school heroine, here I come!

Except I didn't have a chance.

Someone knew someone from my previous school and gossip of my mole, and the botched removal attempt, became the new school joke. It took no time for mortifying "before and after" photos to make the rounds, and the fact that I'd lied about how I got the scar turned everyone against me. Not one student would even talk to me. Their hateful emotions seeped into me like poison, chilling my veins, making me ill.

I hadn't escaped.

I wish I could turn my powers off, to just ignore all those emotions for just a second. Or turn them back the other way and make everyone else know how I was feeling. Because right now, walking down this school corridor with my chin up pretending to smile was the hardest thing in the world.

My eyes stung. No way, if I cried in the middle of everyone, it was all over.

I turned to face the wall and got lucky. There was a notice board right there, covered in fluoro fliers for me to pretend to read while I got myself under control. There were fliers for cheerleading try-outs, chess clubs and the whole spectrum of other cliques that wouldn't take me.

Just breathe.

The corridor stank of bleach from a recent cleaning. If anyone saw my eyes damp and asked if I was OK, I'd say my eyes were sensitive to the chemicals. I always had an answer for everything. I just needed someone to ask.

I closed my eyes, and when I opened them again, Rafael, who I'd already identified as the most handsome guy *ever*, was leaning next to me. He had one elbow against the wall and his hand played with his sun-bleached hair. I don't blame him; my hands would love to do that, too.

Rafael had the looks of a 1950's movie star and he knew it. He played it up, wearing a leather jacket with turned-up collar like he was James Dean and said things like doll, daddy-o, and swell. Yeah, I've been eaves-stalking. Just a bit.

And here he was next to me, looking at me. What was going on? I scanned my surroundings for hidden cameras.

"Since you're new, I'll give you some advice." He spoke in my ear, closer than I'm used to anyone getting. I shivered.

"Advice?"

"Don't join the chess club," he said.

I let what must be a dumbfounded expression stay on my face and spoke slowly. "But... the checkered boards are so pretty, and I like the little horsies."

Rafael looked at me like I was a poor dumb girl and I worried I'd missed my shot. I raised an eyebrow dramatically, hoping he got the point.

A moment passed, then he chuckled at my joke and I let out a massive sigh. Internally. Externally, I kept my cool and gave a flirty-yet-coy grin. I was stupidly proud of myself. Maybe I could do this. I could be funny and charming and fab-u-lous. I was beautiful on the inside, and he would be the first person to see. And really, I'd kick ass in chess club, but I'd never let him know that.

"I'm Raf. That's the other important thing you need to know, new girl."

"Emma," I said. I extended a hand to shake his, leaving just one to hold up my books. They shifted, almost fell, and I rebalanced them in a way that squished my boobs up into prominence.

"Oops!" I giggled as though I hadn't done the whole thing on purpose. His smile in return was hungry, almost predatory. I could sense the lusty excitement in him, but also something chilling, a darker emotion hidden under his grin.

"Careful, you'll need those, for, you know, learning."

"No problem. I can shake hands *and* balance books. Get me a job in the circus, I have the skills."

The bell rang. Too soon… I didn't want my time with Rafael to end. This was the nicest anyone had ever been to me and my heart raced with hope and confusion and the close proximity to hottest guy in the world.

Rafael sighed as the bell finished clanging. "Better move. I don't want to get you in trouble on your first day."

Right. I'd been here two weeks. Well, he's noticed me now at least. I had to give him a reason to remember me. Dare I?

"I don't mind getting into trouble sometimes, if it's for a good enough reason."

Raf bumped his shoulder into mine. "You're a firecracker, aren't you? Say, you want to meet up after class? Hang out?"

My lips trembled. "Sure."

"Come to Siren's Haven. You know it?"

I nodded, casually, like I went there all the time. Siren's Haven was an abandoned set of a failed pirate movie, still standing down by the river. I knew all about it because Dad was big into collecting movie props. Tacky replicas mostly, but real stuff too when he could.

"See you there at six, at the main pirate ship. It'll be a gas." Rafael winked at me then headed off down the corridor.

This was too good to be true. I hated that I doubted this, doubted that there could be anything about me he'd find attractive. I was about to split apart, torn between hope and suspicion.

Too jittery for class, I skipped out, went to the girl's bathroom, and did the Snoopy Dance.

Between when I talked to Rafael and the time for our meet up, everything changed. I almost didn't go. I almost curled into a ball of sobbing tears never to face the world again. Then I came up with my plan.

I took so long trying to decide what to wear that I risked being late. I ended up staying in what I wore to school that day: sneakers, black stockings with enough carefully manufactured runs to look everyday, short shorts, and an oversized dusty-red sweater. I'd spent long enough picking it out in the morning anyway and I didn't want to look like I was trying too hard by having an all new outfit on. All I did was change my bra. I also had other preparing to do, and the loose-fitting sweater worked well with my plan.

Twilight lit the fake pirate town, turning grayed wood and dusty weeds varying shades of lilac. I squeezed through the hole in the chain link fence and when my top snagged on one of the cut wires I had a mini panic attack while getting my outfit in order again, covering up what the sweater hid.

I couldn't lose the shakes that had been with me since my conversation with Rafael. They only grew as I made my way to the half-built pirate ship, propped up on blocks down the path. Used spray-cans littered the road like a rainbow and I kicked them along to try and distract my nerves.

Siren's Haven had been abandoned a year ago when issues with actor contracts tanked production. They closed up shop and left it all standing while they tried to get back on track, but in the meantime it had become a playground. I climbed up the weathered wooden ladder onto the ship's deck. Empty beer cans lay scattered around the remains of fires. A couple of old lounges had been dragged in. All the signs of a regular party destination for parties I never got invited to.

Rafael waited for me, reclining on top of a cluster of barrels like a real swashbuckler.

"Hey, sweet cheeks." He rolled onto his side, shifted over, and patted the spot next to him.

"Hey." I strolled across the deck and paused at the barrels. A foam mattress had been thrown on top of them. It made squishy noises when he moved. Ew.

"Come on, don't be shy." Raf patted the mattress again and its moldering stench reached me.

"No pressure, I'm not going to try anything. I'm a gentleman."

I already knew how untrue that statement was. But even still, I wanted to give him the benefit of the doubt. Some dumb part of me still hoped that what I'd overheard wasn't true. For the part of me that despite everything hadn't yet turned bitter, I had to let this play out.

"Can I admit something?" My voice quavered, but that was ok, I was aiming for cute and vulnerable. But really I was super nervous about what was going to happen. "I haven't been here before. I want to have a look around. Can you show me?"

"A tour? Sure, doll, sure." He hopped down onto the deck with a smooth jump.

The wood squeaked in warning under us, fragile and not meant to have lasted this long. Rafael put an arm around my shoulder and led me to the prow. I hadn't expected him to touch me. My heart thudded. If he had put his arm around my waist the game would have been over.

From the prow of the ship you could see the whole film set. There were mermaids carved into the front wall of the pirate bar (which, like most of the buildings, only had a front wall). Tall grass sprouted everywhere, even from the façades themselves. There was a fake rock pool to our left, and the place might have been pretty if it weren't crumbling and trashed.

"Beautiful, isn't it?" Rafael breathed heavily into my ear. "But not as beautiful as you."

Where did this guy get his lines? I hated that they still made my heart race, even though I had no reason to believe him. Before I could mutter the obvious denial, he kissed me.

It was a small kiss on my temple, soft and a little cheeky. I lost my breath.

"Hey," he said, and turned me toward him. I let him move me as he wished. He smiled down at me and it was a beautiful smile. His emotions told me how excited he was. Excited, and smug.

He whispered in my ear. "Take your top off for me."

The last fine cobweb of hope I'd clung to snapped. I knew this was coming, but I clung anyway, and now I felt myself fall. I could stop this and leave now, or I could follow through with the plan I had stupidly dreamed that I wouldn't have to use. Rafael saw my pause and misread my internal conflict.

"It's OK, you're beautiful. I just want to see you."

I nodded slowly and grabbed the bottom hem of my sweater, lifting it up over my head.

I heard the cla-click sound effect of his camera app as I dropped my sweater to the ground.

The hidden camera finally revealed.

He held up his phone, admiring the photo he had taken. "Grade-school underwear, much?"

I had changed out my nice bra that afternoon for a plain black sports tank that covered as much of me as possible. I came prepared. I reached around to the back waistband of my shorts while he examined his photography.

He stood there, still pointing the phone at me, playing his cruel trick.

And I stood, pointing a gun right back.

Checkmate.

"What are you doing? Are you crazy?" He took a clumsy step back and looked around as though there'd be someone to save him.

"I knew. I knew what you had planned!"

After he first talked to me and I danced like a happy fool, thinking he actually wanted me, the fear that it couldn't be true took over. So I went to find Rafael, to follow him and find out more. I knew there had to be something going on with him, and I daydreamed that he just had some cool, dark secret that only I could know, like he had freaky powers too, or he really was from the 1950's. Instead it turned out that he was simply a jerk.

“I heard you talking to Gavin. Saying you had me eating out of your hands, and you were going to get a photo to blackmail me with to make me do whatever you wanted.” I jabbed the gun at him as I talked, my voice growing louder.

“I knew about it all, and even then, I still hoped maybe you were just saying that to your guy as a cover but you really did want…”

I shook my head. I had to stop saying stupid stuff in front of him, as though I were still waiting for him to reveal he cared for me.

No. I had my plan. I knew this was coming, despite any crazy hopes I held. I came here knowing what I would do so that I’d come out of this on top either way.

“Throw your phone over,” I said.

He did, and I deleted the photo of me.

Rafael trembled visibly. His expression was frozen but with my powers, his fear was tangible to me. He had his hands raised in front of him. I pulled out *my* phone and flicked on the camera. Set it to video and kept the gun aimed at him with the other hand.

“I want you to tell the world, Raf, what a jerk you are. A horrible bully. Come on, I’m easy pickings, right? Go for the girl with the mangled face, why don’t you.”

His jaw moved, but he said nothing.

"Say it!"

"I... I'm a jerk, and a bully."

"You are. You take advantage of girls. Say it."

"I take advantage of girls."

The fear flowing off him made me giddy. I hadn't felt such an intense emotion before and it filled me with energy. A grin spread on my face.

"You're nothing but a small-dicked, derivative, misogynistic coward..."

He repeated me on cue.

"Who is about to *die*."

I squeezed the trigger and Rafael twisted like he could dodge a bullet. He couldn't even dodge the spray of water shooting from the gun. Working replica water pistols formed a large part of my Dad's prop collection.

Not all the wet on Rafael was from the gun. His pants were soaked. I giggled as I turned the video off on the phone and slipped it into my shorts pocket.

"Wow, a better performance than I could have hoped for. Now listen carefully, Mr. Popular. You're going to be my new bestest friend at school. You'll help show everyone how fab-u-lous I can be. Because if you don't, I will show everyone who you *really* are."

My plan complete, I turned to strut away, the proud victor.

I felt the change before I saw anything. The fear gushing from Rafael shifted to blinding fury. The heavy sound of footfalls charged at me.

He shoved me hard from behind and I landed on my face. The aged wood deck grazed my hands, turning them into splinter pincushions. I rolled onto my back, looking up at him. The anger on his face was terrifying, the strongest anger I'd ever sensed.

"No one is going to see that video, ugly bitch!"

He reached down, grabbing at the pocket of my shorts.

I wrestled against his hands, swatting him away.

"No way are you blackmailing me. You're going to suffer."

He slapped me in the face.

Something strange was happening with my powers. I felt Rafael's anger flow down onto me, bathing me, seeping into my muscles and warming them. I felt strong, the same strength I felt when I broke that girl's arm. The splinters didn't bother me. My cheek felt hot where Rafael had slapped me, but didn't sting. I felt powerful.

Rafael swung at me again and I knocked his arm away easily. He pulled back, shocked, and nursed his arm where I hit it.

I knew then I was stronger than him. My powers had always felt like a curse before, but now I realized they were something more. I was something superhuman.

I leapt onto my feet, grinning and staring Rafael down. He shied away from me.

That's where I should have left it. I should have made some witty comment, and walked away. But my hands balled into fists, wanting more fight. With this strength running through me I felt out of control. I wanted revenge for every painful word or look I'd ever suffered.

I kicked high and hard, hitting Rafael right in the centre of his chest.

He *flew* backward, like he was wired up for a movie stunt.

I was a witch after all.

Rafael hit the figurehead at the prow of the boat with a sound that made me feel sick. I instantly regretted lashing out, and went to help him up, to make sure nothing was broken. Even if he was a jerk, I hated myself for being so violent.

I took one step and a squealing groan came from the ship, followed by popping and cracking noises of wood splitting. I felt the deck shudder, and knew the ship would fall.

I looked at Rafael, groaning as he tried to get back on his feet. My body screamed with energy. I felt strong, fast, and confident, like I could reach him, throw him over my shoulder, and leap to safety in time. But he was so far away, all the way at the other end of the ship, where I had kicked him to.

The ship lurched to the side as the hull split open and I ran for him. I leaped over holes that tore open in the deck. Something huge fell into my field of vision and I saw the main mast collapse down into my path, right in front of me. Unable to handle my new speed, I slammed into it and rolled to the side. My momentum spun me too fast and I fell from the side of the ship, tumbling to the ground.

Coughing dirt, all I could do was watch as the pirate ship collapsed in on top of Rafael.

I bolted away from Siren's Haven before the dust settled. I had to sneak back inside so my parents wouldn't see that I'd lost my sweater and come home half-dressed.

It wasn't my fault. It was my fault. It wasn't my fault. It was my fault. My brain was stuck in a loop of guilt and denial. There were too many variables, but I knew one thing—if I had held back, if I hadn't let my anger loose, Rafael might still be alive.

I deleted my video of Rafael for fear it could be used as evidence against me. I fretted about the sweater I'd left behind and hoped it would be considered just another piece of trash, not a clue to a crime. I plotted various excuses and alibis for if I was questioned. I had answers for everything.

But no one came for me.

A week later, I went to the funeral.

The grief I felt from Rafael's family ached, pounding into my skull, and I told myself it was the punishment I deserved. But not everyone grieved. Two rows in front of me, gleeful relief came from a small huddle of girls from school. I wondered what Rafael had done to them, whether they were on a long list of blackmail victims. I tried to cheer myself up by pretending I was a hero who saved those girls from Rafael's conniving schemes. But it didn't work. No matter what he did, I knew he didn't deserve to die. Heroes bring people to justice, not beat them up and fail to save them.

After the ceremony, I wandered through the crowded church, exploring the mix of emotions held by the funeral-goers. Some kids from school just thought it was cool to be there, since Rafael was so popular. His death made big news, and parents were already lobbying to have the "death trap" film set demolished. They all believed it was an accident, and nothing could have been done. I was the only person who knew that wasn't true. My brain played through hundreds of alternate endings for the night if I'd made different choices. I wish it would stop. I couldn't take back the choices I'd made.

There were a couple of guys I didn't know drifting through the funeral crowd, taking donations for some vague anti-teen-death charity. They looked like brothers. Both had the same cute, roguish charm. Their faces showed commiseration, but my powers told me they felt smug, the same kind of smug Rafael had felt as he pulled his trick. I wondered just what trick these two were up to. Every single person gave them money. A LOT of money. I watched with interest from a quiet corner.

Gavin, Rafael's best friend and blackmail confidant, found me there.

"You were with him, weren't you?" His voice was a growl.

I acted shocked. "Me and Rafael? Why would *he* have been somewhere with *me*?"

"I know he was going to meet you. You had something to do with him dying, I know it. You've been acting weird all week. Why were your hands all scratched up? What happened?"

He loomed over me. I saw anger in him, bubbling under his skin like the glow of lava. But now I knew what I could do with someone else's anger. I couldn't let him reveal to anyone I was with Rafael that night. I had to scare him off and I had the power to do it.

"I don't know what you're talking about," I drawled. I rested a hand on the crossbar of a stone crucifix next to me. "But whatever happened to him could happen to you too if you don't keep quiet and leave me alone."

I squeezed my grip and the stone crumbled like chalk. The patter of the pieces falling to the floor was covered by the talking crowd. Gavin looked at me like the freak I was. My demonstration clearly had the desired effect.

Gavin ran away, leaving me with my regrets. Was I really a witch, or a monster? Was that the path I was fated for, using my powers for evil? I started to wonder how much I could achieve with my newfound abilities. Maybe, one way or another, I could still turn my life around.

The older boy with the donation bucket stared at me. I stared back, waiting for him to glance to my scar, be disgusted and turn away. My glare was a challenge.

But instead he smiled.

He came over and introduced himself. His name was Jake, and he was there with his little brother Jamie. They'd read about the funeral in the newspaper and came to see what donations they could get for their own "charitable cause".

"I saw what you just did," Jake whispered, dramatically low considering no one was interested in our conversation anyway. He kicked at the broken stone on the floor and raised his eyebrows.

"I didn't do anything. It was dodgy craftsmanship, broke on its own."

"You're a fast thinker, too. Perfect," he said. "Don't worry, I know what you can do, because I can do it, too. I'm so glad I spotted you. It's rare to find someone special, like us. How about we get out of here and talk more. Doesn't all this sadness give you a headache?"

I couldn't stop my eyes widening. "You really feel it too?"

Jake grinned. "The emotion reading, the super strength, the whole deal."

The idea of other people with powers like mine made a strong need for belonging bloom in my chest. My voice sounded way too vulnerable when I asked, "Can you help me understand what I am?"

"Sure. Come with me. I want to tell you how sticking by me will give you everything you ever wanted. Everything that people like us deserve."

Every nerve inside me ached to go with Jake, my body rebelling against my better judgment. Jake was charming and so handsome it made my palms sweaty. There was something downright supernatural about how tempting he was, but also something wrong and disturbing. I wouldn't fall for sweet talk again, and could already tell he wasn't one of the good guys.

I shook my head. "No. Go away. You're not my type."

Jake looked stunned. I doubt he got turned down… ever. He stared, assessing me again, his gaze lingering on my face.

He handed me a business card.

"What's this?" I asked.

"A gift, something I'm guessing is high on your wish list. I'll let Dr Rachenko know you're coming and to put any work on my tab. I've written my number on the back so you can get in touch again when you've seen what I can do for you."

I stared at the card. *Dr Rachenko- Discreet cosmetic surgery and enhancements.*

Jake tapped the card as I held it in my hands. "Everything you ever wanted starts here."

Jake called his brother over and the two of them left the building, counting the money they had been collecting from the grieving crowd. Definitely not on the good guy side.

I stared at what Jake had given me, my fingers clenched and shaking around the thin cardboard. Jake had offered me a new life, a new skin, and all I could wonder was what trick he would play on me, what catch this promise held. I couldn't stand the idea that his offer wasn't true.

And if the only catch was that I wouldn't be one of the good guys either, could I do that?

Deep inside I had always wanted to be something good and special, but it seems that I was born to be something other than a hero. I never had that sort of strength in me, the strength to stay beautiful on the inside. Ugliness had crawled inside me, driven in by the cruel words and games of my peers. It sat there, next to the dull ache I felt in my chest whenever my mind replayed the night at Siren's Haven. A montage it chose to replay often.

I shook the guilt and regret away, denying it. It didn't matter anymore. I would become beautiful on the outside. Everything I wanted, I would take. I had great plans. Operation: New Me, Mark II would not fail.

The End

AUTHOR'S NOTE

When I decided to write Emma's backstory, I knew that it was going to be the tragic origin of a villain, rather than the normal hero's tale. That's the sort of story I'm used to writing, and that we're all used to reading- a person surmounting all the terrible trials thrown at them to become something better. In my mind, the difference between good people and bad people are the decisions they make in their darkest moments. Not everyone has it in them to rise above, and it's the ones that fall, that are beaten down, that tragically become villains. That's the story I wanted to explore in Emotionally Scarred. I don't want readers to think that Emma's actions are to be condoned, despite Rafael being not too nice himself. Emma has it in her to become a true super-villain. Will she, or will she have a chance to redeem herself?

Thanks for reading my short story, I hope you enjoyed it. You can read more about Emma and whether her "Operation: New Me, Mark II" plan succeeds and how she has to deal with what she's done in other books from the Empath Chronicles series.

ABOUT THE AUTHOR

Born in 1981 to Australian and Maltese parents, Selina lives in Australia with her husband, daughter and an unnamed cat. During her life Selina has found ancient Roman treasure, survived cancer, had knights joust at her wedding, been mugged for doughnuts, made a living as a visual artist and eaten every bizarre and wonderful food put in front of her. And now she writes stories.

FIND OUT MORE ABOUT SELINA AT HER WEBSITE-
WWW.SELINAFENECH.COM

ALSO BY SELINA FENECH

MEMORY'S WAKE

AN ILLUSTRATED FANTASY NOVEL FOR YOUNG ADULTS.

WWW.MEMORYSWAKE.COM

Lost in a world full of monstrous fairies, a troubled sixteen year old has to find out who she is and why her memories were stolen before she is found by those who want her dead.

She takes the name "Memory" and knows she has just one goal - to find her way home, wherever that is. But this land is strange. No technology to be seen, and iron is banned, thanks to a pact the humans have with the magical creatures who share their pre-industrial era world. In her t-shirt and torn jeans, Memory knows she's different, even before she performs impossible magic.

Haunted by her past, chased by a dragon, wanted by the king and stalked by the strange, handsome savage that seems to know her, everyone is after Memory, and she suspects it's not just for her eye-catching outfit. Her forgotten past holds dangerous secrets that will challenge everything she believes and risk the lives of everyone she loves.

A THANK YOU TO MY READERS

Thank you for reading my story, it means a lot to me to be sharing my imaginary worlds with others. As an indie author, receiving reviews and seeing people talk about my books are my favorite things, like receiving a big warm hug from my readers! Reviews also help me improve as an author, so your opinions matter. Writing a review is fast and easy, so please consider returning to the website you purchased this book and leaving a review. If you've enjoyed my story, tell your friends. They might like it too, and it's more fun when you can talk about a story with your friends!

If you want to discuss the story or make sure I see your comments, just drop me an email at selina@selinafenech.com. I love to hear from readers, and reply to all personal emails!

55466651R00093

Made in the USA
Lexington, KY
23 September 2016